Industrial Carpet Drag

Bruce Taylor

Bizarro Pulp Press
an imprint of JournalStone Publishing

Bizarro Pulp Press books may be ordered through booksellers or by contacting:

Bizarro Pulp Press, a JournalStone imprint
www.BizarroPulpPress.com

The views expressed in this work are solely those of the authors and do not necessarily reflect the views of the publisher, and the publisher hereby disclaims any responsibility for them.

ISBN: 978-0-69-224078-6

Printed in the United States of America
JournalStone rev. date: October 13, 2014

Cover Art: Jim Agpalza
Cover Design by: Lori Michelle
Interior Formatting by: Lori Michelle
www.theauthorsalley.com

☠Praise for Bruce Taylor

" . . . a very gifted short fiction writer."
—Jeff VanderMeer,
three-time winner, thirteen-time finalist for the
World Fantasy Award.

"The transformational figure for science fiction."
—Elton Elliott,
former editor of *The Science Fiction Review* and
co-editor, *Like Water for Quarks*.

"It's important to realize that Bruce's stories are not strange; the world is and he's separated himself from it in order to show us new realities, with remarkable clarity and insight. I am one of his admirers and I am not alone."
—Brian Herbert,
New York Times bestselling author and co-author
with Kevin J. Anderson, the *Dune series*.

"A writer of imagination and insight, Bruce Taylor delivers a collection of stories that amazes and intrigues."
—Terry Brooks,
New York Times bestselling author.

In memoriam: To Jay Lake—fine friend, great writer. Though you left us far too early, what you did while you were here, as person and as a writer—was spectacular. And for your generous words about my work, especially the wonderful introduction to *Edward: Dancing on the Edge of Infinity*—my gratitude and appreciation knows no bounds. Thank you! Thank you and a million times: Thank you! And I will *SO* miss you.

And to the Literary Lions of our time:

To Ray Bradbury: Your kind words about my work so long ago was so appreciated and so encouraging (and then to actually meet you!) Thank you! And your work, showing how lyricism can turn genre into poetry: inspirational as it was profound. But above all, thank you for giving permission to own and delight— in one's imagination! If your soul is in a world beyond this one, may it be the world of *The Martian Chronicles*, in an elegant sandship, slipping across the sandy, silent floors of the vanished seas of Mars.

To Gabriel Garcia Marquez: thank you for magic realism and defining the dreamscape of what we call reality. (And that maybe magic realism is, in fact, 'code' for reality?) Wherever your spirit is now, may it be honored, enfolded, and gently carried in a cloud of yellow butterflies.

INTRODUCTION

On the surface, you might think that reading a story by Bruce Taylor is going to be fun, a light romp through the universe of magic realism. He is, after all, Mr. Magic Realism, and many of the images he conjures up are downright funny. I have been known to laugh until I cry at some of his marvelous, whimsical descriptive passages, such as one he wrote about a talking, dancing computer keyboard, and Dina Shore singing as she drove through Incan ruins in a 1956 Chevrolet Bel Air—passages that we included in one of our collaborative stories, "Under Burning Skies."

The Bruce Taylor story you are about to read—*Industrial Carpet Drag*—is quite humorous, but only to a degree. The author uses humor to talk about very important issues, so that it doesn't sound like he is preaching to his readers. Taken as a whole, this is one of the most serious pieces Bruce has ever written. It is a journey of discovery into a fantastic realm—one that is both internal and external, a trip into the nether-reality between waking consciousness and the partial-awareness of dreams.

The protagonist, Bryce, is a sane man in an insane world, and is filled with anxiety. He fears that he's been poisoned by the off-gassing of carpets, paint, sealants, and glues in his home. He's learned that the toxic fumes from such products can cause memory loss, anxiety, depression numbness, slurred speech, and seizures, and can bring on a syndrome known as multiple chemical sensitivity. He's also concerned about the plastic bottles he's been drinking liquids from, because he's heard that a chemical used in plastics leaches into water, and can disrupt human hormones.

On his journey, Bryce seeks knowledge from everyone he encounters, including characters from literature such as Oedipus and the Cheshire cat of *Alice In Wonderland*, and from film, such as Dr. Morbius of *Forbidden Planet*. Bryce rides on the back of a huge dragonfly and has an animated conversation with Mr. Blaklavach, a foolish creature who resembles an eight-eyed spider and loses his eyes one by one under the assault of Bryce's anger, until at last he only has two left—thus pointing to the human aspect of this creature.

There is also Mr. Dinglepood, who is upset because he says he came up with the concept of the unconscious power of the human mind, the Id, that Sigmund Freud received credit for. Even so, Mr. Dinglepood provides our protagonist with advice for the journey he is taking, a journey that at times is more like a dream—but as Bruce Taylor points out so profoundly: "Dreams may be messages. The back door to insight."

Here then is a journey of self-discovery for the protagonist, Bryce, and a journey to understand the human condition, and how it has so adversely affected the environment of our planet—and what can be done to improve both. It is a journey from despair and hopelessness to hope and beauty, to the knowledge that each person contains the seeds of Shakespearean brilliance, and the ability to do what Rachel Carson called for in her environmental writings. And the overpopulated, polluted Earth, despite all that mankind has done to harm it, still has incredible wilderness areas, including ones Bruce Taylor and I have hiked into, such as the stunningly beautiful Enchantment Lakes and the Necklace Valley, both in the North Cascade mountain range in Washington state.

The weather is wild, wacky and out of control in this story, with freak tornadoes where they shouldn't be, massive lightning bolts, torrential rain, and huge hail stones. Much of this is linked, in Bryce's view, to global warming caused by our industrial society's air pollution. Even the weather girl on television, who should be a helpful authority figure, seems oddly out of place. To Bryce, she appears to be nineteen and living in a sorority. She's blond-haired and as brainless as a turnip. At one point Bryce goes out on a balcony and is shocked to see that the buildings of the city of Seattle are all upside down. So much seems out of control as he continues his journey that it's a wonder he survives as long as he does. But survive he does, and he learns many things along the way. He laments the helplessness of the human condition, how people are buffeted this way and that by extreme weather, greedy corporations, careless people, and stupid people whom you are forced to depend on.

Filled with concerns about the rampant environmental damage caused by our civilization, including the dangers of plastics, the story's protagonist meets a strange, plastic-bottle-shaped creature, Mr. Sev N, who has a psychotic disdain for the environment. He hates Rachel Carson in particular, because of all she did to enhance our awareness of this planet, in *The Silent Spring* and in her other sentinel works. Bryce tries to learn what he can from even such an odd, destructive creature as Mr. Sev N, and then he moves on.

One of the most interesting and poignant characters you will meet in this story is a little girl who sits in a white robe, watching the planet Earth spin slowly before her. With a deep and abiding sadness she watches the polar ice caps shrinking and oceans flashing into steam as the Earth becomes molten, but she also sees the lovely flash of sunlight on the seas and on the white swirls of clouds. The identity of this child is not revealed until the end of the story—and even that ending is not an ending, because we are left with something that we have learned from the strength of the author's writing, an awareness that we must take personal actions that are significant and important for the sake of this world. If we don't do that, we are sealing not the only the fate of the planet, but the fate of ourselves as a species. It will all be gone.

Ultimately, through all the travails faced by the protagonist in this story, and Bruce Taylor's light touch with humor, I can't help thinking of what a friend said to me once. He had spent a lifetime studying Buddhism and traveling the world, looking for answers that would improve his life, and the lives of others around him. With a bemused expression, my friend paraphrased a teaching of Buddha, putting it like this: "When you see what it is all about, there will be nothing left to do except to have a good laugh."

Brian Herbert

Seattle, Washington
March 17, 2014

☠.1.

So you help Stan move into his new townhouse. Stan, he's a green-eyed burly guy with a crew cut and tattoos on his arm, one of which looks like poison nightshade winding its way up a dagger on the blade of which reads, "9/11— The Truth" and he's got these real muscular arms that make him look like he's been body-building all of the nine months before the day he popped out into the world and eyes so intense that it makes you think he sees a conspiracy in everyone who walks and talks and barks and purrs and tweets. You look at him and what really stands out is the angular nature of the face and the pointy jaw that looks like the absolute wrong head was screwed on this body like what really belongs there is an older version of a cherubic face replete with roughened skin, scene of ancient acne wars, but that's neither here nor there.

What's here is that it's moving day, it's hotter n' shit and it's not even noon but you're helping Stan move into this townhouse that's all brand new with this fucking awesome view of downtown Seattle, Lake Union, Mt. Rainier and you wonder how he pulled it off because you never knew in all the years you've known him for him to be so fucking rich. How could you miss that? You go back to junior high school, been buds forever, even dormed together at the U of W. *God, you think, how you can know someone forever but—not know much about them after all*? You ponder this when you're sitting on the second floor deck off the living room, taking a break from hauling up the bed frame to the third floor and leaving the moving truck open. ("Wallingford is a pussy place," he says, "everyone knows everyone. No one gets into your pants or nothin'.")

And given how he sees a conspiracy in everything, you wonder how he can be so trusting with moving this expensive shit that he just bought at Mor Furniture.

Anyway, you and him sit there on some red plastic "Vita-Gold" dairy cases, you know—the kind they haul milk in with the triangular open framework for Lite-weight! Strength! as you guess advertising copy would put it, and you and Stan have a Moosedrool as you look out over the city on that bright clear day in early June, a month of great weather, a respite from that rotten winter with the three storms of 100 mph winds and loads of rain which washed away parts of I-5 for twenty miles in each direction and you know it's global warming and Stan says that's a crock of shit, that mankind can't be doing that, it's just earthly wobble around an increasingly sweaty sun and you wonder again about just how localized his conspiracy-laden mind is—can't be any disinformation from ExxonMobile about carbon dioxide, can it? Naw. Just a wobble in the Earth's axis. And anyway, you sit there drinking beer, admiring the killer view, secretly hating Stan and you start sneezing.

Industrial Carpet Drag

Stan looks at you.

You sneeze and sneeze and sneeze and Stan says, "Whoa, man, I didn't know you had allergies."

You start coughing. "I didn't either."

"Huh," he says. "Never?"

"Had some when I was a kid, but got over 'em, though in the last couple of years had some real bad colds but not allergies—" You pause, "I don't think— wow," you say. "Weird. Don't know where this is comin' from."

He takes a drink. You smell the intoxicating aroma of fresh paint and another nose flavor you can't really identify but you wonder if it's that deep blue carpeting that looks like it's as thick as grass and you admire and hate Stan again 'cause everyday he's gonna be tickling his toesies into that rug turf while you, back at your third-floor rental place, wouldn't dream of doing that with your ancient coffee-stained, food-stained carpeting and that thought makes you think even more dismally about your apartment—the walls that haven't been painted in the God knows how many years you've been there plus your great view of 42nd and 12th in the U-District and not much more beyond that save the apartment across from you where, if you're real careful, you can lay on the couch in the living room where the window ledge is just several feet or so above the floor and you can look down and into that apartment across the street and with a good pair of binoculars, watch that couple fucking on the living room floor and you smirk. Hey, Stan doesn't have a view of that. But with Peggy, he doesn't need that but you'd still trade your voyeurism for a view of Seattle and Mt. Rainier. Oh, yeah, Lake Union, too. Shit.

Stan sneezes. And sneezes. And coughs. "Wow," he says. "So what's with the sudden hay fever? Musta caught it from you."

"Dunno," you say. Then, "Well buddy, you got yourself a sweetheart deal."

What you really wanna say is, "OK. How'd you do it? Rich uncle? What?" It's impolite to ask. That's what your daddy always said. So he ended up assuming he knew it all. Smug in his intelligence how he could get information without being direct. And usually, mostly always wrong, but you never looked at that. You just look at when he was right—well, that's the only time it mattered to him. Even if it was only 2% of the time. Oh, well—neh-ver mind.

But Stan is smug. A fresh wind blows in from the south and you can smell someone's lilacs in bloom and you forget that you two were just sneezing your heads off and Stan takes a drink of Moosedrool and says, "Pays to have contractors and bankers in your family."

You don't have to wonder anymore. No siree. Not at all. Matter of fact, you hope to crap he doesn't say anything else about it 'cause now you know. It's to your great ire that you know this because it reminds you of the people you didn't have and wished you had in your family and now you kinda wish you hadn't wanted to know after all and maybe Stan won't say much more—but—

But—he goes on. It gets worse.

"Yeah, ol' Uncle Charlie made a killing off the other three of these town homes and because I'm his favorite, gave me a sweetheart deal. Shhh. Don't tell nobody. Forty percent off."

You guess. You're pretty good at mental math; you

Industrial Carpet Drag

saw the flyer. 410K. *Lessee,* you calculate—*forty percent— that's, let's see—ten percent is 41K so four times that—oh, holy shit—oh crap* you think, *even I could have afforded that—164K off the price means he got it at—um—410 minus 164 equals 246! TWO FORTY SIX!* You scream inside your head. *Fucking shit! 1600 square feet, double garage, three bedroom, 2 and 1/2 bath* YOU HATE STAN *stainless steel kitchen. Granite counter tops, good lookin' paint and rugs AH CRAP!*

And it gets MUCH worse. You don't know how bad it gets till you see Stan scooch back the crate chair he's sitting on so he can lean back against the siding next to the state-of-the-art green technology vinyl framed, sliding glass door off the living room. He takes a drink of beer, grins in triumph and says with great satisfaction, "Mom's brother got me a four percent loan and Mom gave me the down payment. So I'm paying on $199,000 so it comes out to about 800 a month." He sighs, smiles. "Not bad."

You're happy for him, glum for yourself. Your rent is $810 a month. $810 a month for a crummy old one-bedroom apartment with eentsy-teensy bathroom, and maybe 500 square feet. And you don't want to admit to yourself that it's not Stan who you're really pissed at. If you copped to that, you don't know who you'd even begin with.

"However—" says Stan, "however—" and he looks at you a long time. "Gosh, you know, all this house—and even me and Peggy, still too much house for us—maybe—" and he looks away, and you don't know if he's taking in the view of Seattle or the sky or The Mountain, "Maybe—gosh—maybe—maybe I could have a roommate—'specially since Peggy and I gotta travel a lot—" He continues to kinda look away and he says, "Don't suppose you know of anyone who would want to pay 400 a month for a room—do you—? Y'know, share this space—y'know, someone who likes *Star Trek*, *Twilight Zone*, Bizarro writing, Kafka and you know—"

Suddenly you stop hating Stan. You laugh. You turn. You smile. "Can't think of anyone—" you say, "outside myself."

Stan grins. "Huh," he says. "I'm so surprised. That was easy. Deal?"

"Fuck YES! Deal!"

You clink Moosedrools, drain 'em, have another one. And another one. And somehow amidst lots of laughing and a well-timed fart here and there and lots of sweating, you get all the furniture moved in. There's also lots of sneezing but what the hell. Pollen. What else could it *possibly* be?

☠2.

A week or so later, on another, hot, sunny Saturday, Peggy comes to the townhouse later that afternoon, after her shift at Starbucks. She's the kinda lady that occupies your cum-dreams, tall and silky lady with that long blonde hair, brown eyes and trim and proper. You always envied Stan for having the guts to ask such a gorgeous lady out when you all met at the Mountaineers not long after you and Stan graduated from the U. Looking at her, you'd never guess she could haul a fifty pound backpack up Asgaard Pass to the Upper Enchantment Plateau—("What the hell," she said, "it's only 2000 feet in a quarter mile.") You remember hiking that and she was waaaay fucking ahead of you and you were waaaaay ahead of Stan. When you got to that viewpoint of Snowcreek Glacier, you collapsed, Stan threw up and Peggy sat there taking pictures and eating a Harvest Granola Bar. Even though the Cascades are only the sixth most vertical mountains on the planet from valley bottom to ridge top, as far as you were concerned you just whacked up Everest. God knows how Stan experienced it; maybe like climbing the 97,000 foot Olympus Mons volcano on

Mars with a leaky space suit. But boy, Peggy just sat there humming, munching, taking pictures like she had just taken a walk in the park or a stroll around Seattle's Green Lake.

Anyway, you come back to the here and now and she glides through the door, flops her black shoulder bag on the granite kitchen counter, trots over to Stan and gives him a kiss on the lips which turns into a mutual tongue job, then gives him a loooong squeeze and says, "Hey happy new homeowner, let's admire the place again." Then she comes over to you and says, "Lucky you, Bryce, lucky, lucky you. What an offer to share this yum-place with Mr. Macho Man and he lay-dee fren'. You so lucky." She gives you a hug, smooches you on the cheek and then says, "I'm so glad you said yes to the offer."

"Oh, yeah," you say, "oh, yeah. Offer I couldn't refuse." You three then go back downstairs and stand there on the entry floor looking past the door to the garage, the door to the bathroom, to the big spare bedroom that will soon be filled with your stuff.

"Nice," she says again, "like a suite. Good planning." She sneezes. Sniffs. "Woof," she says, "something detoxing. Probably paint or rugs. It'll be OK in a coupla weeks or so." She looks thoughtful, "Provided they used high-end products."

"Oh," you say, "that's what that is?"

"Oh, yeah," says Peggy looking at you with a bit of a puzzled look like saying, I mean, ain't it obvious? "Ever heard of 'Sick Building Syndrome'?"

You gotta think for a minute. "Oh, yeah—but that was just a bunch of people who being weird wasn't it? I mean—couldn't actually be buildings—"

Peggy shakes her head. "Lots of controversy," she

Industrial Carpet Drag

says, "Manufacturers did everything, do everything they could and can do to squelch the idea that what they were constructing could make people sick."

Stan listens then says, "Well, yeah, class-action lawsuits kinda screw up profits."

Peggy shakes her head again. You love it when she does that, how her hair moves. Lovely lady but, you realize, your last lady was pretty fair too. But she headed off to New York and long distance relationships suck. But there's MaryAnne; you've been getting to know her and she ain't too bad herself.

You point to the room that will be yours—all yours—and you say, "That's where the bed goes, against that far wall so I can look out the sliders to the patio and catch some of the view."

Not a fantastic view. But a view. Sure a lot better than what you're used to but you will miss the scene of the couple screwing in the apartment across the street. Boy, they just loved the living room floor, they seemed to hump for hours and she had those nice boobs—

"—yeah," Peggy was saying, "yeah, well I hope this works well for you."

"Working OK already," you say, "especially, after this place outgases, if that's what it is—I thought it was pollen with the sneezing—though I've been having more colds recently—weird, not long after I turned thirty-two—"

Peggy nods, "I've heard of weird stuff happening to people after they turn thirty-two but who knows. Anyway, just be glad it's been warm and we can keep the place aired out. Supposed to be nice for a while. You'll be OK. They've really cleaned up their act about this outgassing stuff over the years." Then she puts her hands on her hips and looks like she's in charge and surveying a jobsite. "Nice," she says, "this will be really nice." Then she turns to Stan standing there in his paint splotched jeans and the tee shirt with a picture of a cartoon by Gary Larson which shows the inside of a car and a guy looking into the side mirror and huge dangling insect legs behind it and the words that read in the mirror, "Objects in Mirror are closer than they appear." "Let's go upstairs." she says.

You go up those Berber-carpeted steps, carpet that you don't particularly like the color of—kind of a gray-blue but more gray than blue. It isn't bad but somehow it seems cheap and also rough in texture. But it's Stan's place and he loves it.

You go back up to the second floor. You love going up to the second floor—the layout is so fucking amazing. *There are second floors*, you think, *and there are second floors but this second floor is a just plain knockout.* It's no secret. You AB-so-LUTE-ly just covet the place, the plush deep gray-blue carpeting. It isn't Berber. It's something else. PlushplushPLUSH! You just know you're going to love walking around in it like the rug is one great big plush bedroom slipper. The stairway pops you up mid-wall to the second floor—to your right, that fucking amazing kitchen with the black granite countertops, double-sink, Wein-Glaz double-sided stainless steel refrigerator, the matching, smooth-top stove with the Smart-Off feature that senses whether or not a pan is on the burner and shuts it off after five minutes if there is nothing there so you can't possibly leave the stove on and burn the place down as you dash out the door on your way to yet another event of ultimate self-actualization, the Wein-Glaz microwave over the stove with three settings for popcorn, the trash compactor, the dishwasher, the cherry cabinets and alllll the counter space you would *ever* want, plus the island, plusplusplus. God how many pluses can a fucking kitchen have? View over the sink is that of another unit, but who cares 'cause when you turn, oh, holy shit, that vast dining and living room separated by a low wall jutting out from the right-hand wall, with a double-sided fireplace facing living and dining area and the view—and the view and the view and you just canNOT get over the view. Furniture is still in crazy angles all over the place and you and Peggy and Stan move the floral-patterned blue couch in place, against the right wall so you can sit and turn your head slightly to the right and—oh my God—take in—oh holy crap—the Jezhus Christ—view—yikes! Seattle! The works, the billion dollar view. And you think, I GET TO HAVE THIS! HOLY CRAP! DOES IT GET ANY BETTER THAN THIS? WHOOEE LUCKEE MAN—I IS ONE-A LUCKEE MAN!

You spend a few more minutes of reveling in your good fortune sitting on that new, deep blue sofa, the one with the yellow and green floral pattern. ("When I saw that," said Peggy, "I loved it. It so reminded me of the one my Grandmother Landis had.") Though it was a dink-bender and a sphincter-buster to get it up the stairs and to get from the top of the stairs into the room. "Oh," said Stan, "they did a good job with the stairway even though this is kinda tough with the couch—but I've seen places where you have to fucking disassemble the TV to just get it the door." You guessed you were cheered to hear that but it still was a lot of work and you could see Stan watching carefully that the sage colored paint didn't get scritched, scratched or otherwise bloobered.

Bruce Taylor

Anyway, you and Stan then scoot the chairs around, placing one just to the left of the double-sided fireplace in the living room, and after that you put together the seven-piece deep cherry dining set in the area between the fireplace and that fucking! Amazing! Kitchen! out of that History Channel's documentary on *Walt Disney Presents* and the "Tomorrowland" segment of what a futuristic kitchen would have probably looked like as envisioned in the fifties. Maybe. You are not really sure about this but back some years ago, yeah, it would have looked really futuristic with futuristic spelled with a capital F.

Peggy futzes around in the kitchen, placing a big bright orange bowl on the black, granite-topped eating bar facing the dining area and dumps in bananas, apples and oranges that she got from Trader Joe's on her way over from the Starbucks up near 50th and Wallingford, the main drag—the really plush Starbucks with all the soft, cushy seats, Wi-Fi and the baristas smiling a lot because it looked like they were working in a resort, like a top of the line Starbucks with the rough, tan tile on the floor—yeah, you work in a place that nice and then you walk outside and everything else looks like week-old shit, dumped by someone without anything interesting in their diet. Anyway, she continues putting stuff away and then gets out a Teflon-coated frying pan and begins making hamburgers. Stan goes into the kitchen, gives Peggy a smooch on the neck and she giggles and he goes to the fridge and yanks out a couple of Moosedrools. "Sport," he yells, "yo, housemate, onto the deck."

He comes padding over, shoeless, his right red sock has a hole in the toe, and you go out onto the, of course, fucking huge deck, and this time you sit on lawn chairs that have blue plastic pads that won't get soaked by rain and you sit out there sucking on the beer and Stan says, "Dude. Glad to have you here. You pretty well through with that place in the U District?"

"Yeah, just got to get a couple more things out tomorrow, like the bed. This is my last night sleeping there. Getting finished. Just got to vacuum and spiff up the place but I probably won't get much, if any, damage deposit back no matter how much or how little notice I gave—been there six years, place is pretty used."

Stan nods. "Oh, well," he says. He sneezes. "Boy, be glad when this place gets aired out. What time we gonna get together to get this bed stuff taken care of? I can get a truck and we can get your bed, then move the bed from Peggy's place tomorrow." He laughs. "So tomorrow night will be the first night for all of us here. That'll be fun." He leans, yells past the sliding glass door to the interior, "Hey, babe! What time you off tomorrow so we can get our stuff and clear out your place?"

Off in the distance, "—off at two—"

He nods. "'kay—thanks—" He leans back, sucks on the Moosedrool. "Your place, three-thirty?"

"Yup. I don't work tomorrow. Be set and ready to go. Actually, I think I can take the rest of the week off and take care of incidental stuff and get my room set up. They won't miss me too much at VoiceStream." You laugh. "Typical corporation. Expendable."

Stan laughs. "No different at the Lazy B." He laughs again, rubs a hand across his crew cut and then says, "This works. Good." You both sit for a few more minutes, admiring the most! Amazing! View! And you, your great good fortune. It all suddenly looks so good and the future bright and fun. And before long, you have hamburgers, more beer, then fuss and finally give up getting the huge LG plasma TV working. The directions, in English, are incomprehensible; might as well be in Greek. But you know it's gonna be cool when it gets all set up. You look at the box of DVD's on the floor and right on top, a DVD of your favorite movie, *Forbidden Planet*. You smile as you gaze at the image of Robbie the Robot and think, *First time I saw that movie I was ten. Scared the crap out of me. Even now, I still find it freaky*. You put further thoughts of this aside and have another hamburger and a beer.

Later, outside again, you alternately admire your good fortune and Seattle, sparkling in the setting sun.

You sneeze. Once. Twice. And feel a little dizzy. *Must be the glare off the buildings*, you think . . .

☠3.

The mattresses are a wonder and a lesson in incomprehensible awkwardness, as if whoever designed them never had to do anything with them themselves. Getting yours into the lower bedroom is tough enough.

"God," says Stan. "And we have two sets of stairs to get ours up to the third floor." His face is red just from the relatively moderate effort of getting them to your room. Happily, the frame is much easier; just heavy. But you struggle, you endure, and you get the mattress to the third floor, to the bedroom over the living room, the bedroom with the balcony, of course, the vaulted ceilings, the plush carpeting, and of course, the view. It's even more amazing than the second floor.

Stan and Peggy just stand on the balcony, taking it all in. You smile. Nothing to complain about. Nothing at all. Even when Mr. Blaklavach did give you a little something of damage deposit back, you were but when you saw how miserly the amount was, you almost felt insulted. Why even bother?

Blaklavach, in his baggy brown pants, blue plaid

shirt with red suspenders and balding, with thin brown hair turning gray and his little blue eyes looking out though bifocals in thick black frames, somehow always reminding you of what you would imagine an old custodian would look like. He, with those little blue eyes like little cameras zeroed in on every nick, dent, scuff, smooch of marred paint, stain, splotch, no matter, everything he saw was five-dollars-here, ten-dollars-there, and no matter if it hadn't been painted and had been basically ignored for six years, getting nine dollars and fifty cents back from a three-hundred dollar damage deposit was shitty but you realize, *I'll never have to see this fucking passive aggressive dumpy-drawered dolt again.* The knowledge of that, ah, the pleasure. When you left, you kinda wished you could have somehow scuttled back in some way and left a chunk of rotten meat in the refrigerator, just because Blaklavach needed to see how it felt to be on the receiving end.

But, you were out of there now. Though in all honesty, not watching the neighbors across the street fucking—oh, well. Bigger and better things. You consider all of this as you haul the last of the bed frame up to the third floor and Peggy and Stan break their reverie, they're looking out over their future and having everything they ever wanted, and looking at the bright future and so forth and so on, and Peggy comes over, says, "Oh, thank, you—"

"Cool, huh?" says Stan. With his face still red from all the exertion, he points to the five piece fixtures in the bathroom. "Even a bidet for—" he just smiles.

"Watch it," says Peggy, "or I won't let you use it." Pause. "Again." She grins.

Stan laughs, points down the hallway and says,

Industrial Carpet Drag

"So cool. Bathroom, laundry room and the extra bedroom, office suite, whatever—"

Then you hear in your head the voiceover from *Star Trek*, "Space—the final frontier."

By this time, you're already wandering down the hallway again, re-admiring the full bathroom off the hall, carpeted yet, with the washer and dryer behind white, horizontally slatted pocket doors, then the second large bedroom, with a view of the other units and a peek-a-boo view north, toward lush poplars, but on the slant of the roof on the west facing interior wall, a shoulder-high skylight with, of course, a view, facing westward and you can see just a bit of the Olympics Mountains. You shake your head. The contractors didn't miss a beat. Not one thing. You suddenly notice your eyes itching. *Oh, yeah, probably pollen*—though the room has been closed and no windows open. You shake your head.

"Nice office space," you say out loud to yourself.

You can't help but ponder. *$810 a month the last five years, that's*—you shake your head. *Huh. That's easy—it's*—somehow the numbers don't come. You, the mental-math kid and the numbers don't come. You are a bit disturbed by that. You go back into the other bedroom. Stan and Peggy are out on the balcony again, arms around each other's waists—a fresh breeze is blowing in through the open sliders to the balcony and—*snap*—suddenly the numbers just—pop into your head. *Oh, right, yeah—comes out to five x $810 equals*—you stop—*oh, that's right—12 x 810 equals zero, two sixteen plus eight one zero equals nine seven two zero times five equals 48,600 for five years equals—plus probably around 45 grand for the other five years and bang! 93,700 back around eight*

23

years ago would have meant I could have afforded something like this. Why the fuck didn't I buy something, you wonder. *Damn. Before the real estate bubble of '03*—you stop. *No. 2007.* You sigh.

Tinkly-tinkle-tinkle-tingle-cell phone. Peggy's. Mozart's first few bars of—you've heard it a million times—*oh, yeah, yeah*—*"The Jupiter."*

You pick up the phone off the bed and hand it to Peggy who's coming in. That beautiful blond hair, those brown eyes, her grace, and she says, "Thanks," turns away—

Something in her slams on the brakes. "Mom—what's—" she says, "—I—" long pause. Long, long pause. "Oh, my God," she whispers. She sits on the mattress, now in the frame but no covers, no pillows. She leans as if crumbling into the phone.

Stan comes in. Those narrowed eyes. That pensive look. He folds his arms as if he doesn't quite know what to do with them.

"Oh—my God—" is all that Peggy can say, then finally, "—no-no—I had no idea—no—no—we don't have the TV hooked up no I haven't heard anything—oh, my God—is Dad—"

She stands, turns, you see that face and you wonder how many shades of pale a face can have and you wonder where the hell did that blood go—yeah, yeah, that saying about how a person's color can drain away is true. Her color did drain away. She covers the phone, looks at Stan with this incredible look somewhere between imploring, beseeching, bewilderment. She whispers, "Chicago—they're being hit by tornadoes! They've had major damage—" then back to the phone. "Are you OK? Are you OK Oh my God another one—we're coming we're coming we're coming right now Mom? Mom? Mom!"

Industrial Carpet Drag

You three move. Down the stairs, Stan and Peggy grab a suitcase; lots of yelling, "Where is—?" "Get that—" "Leave it—" Lots of frantic dashing here, there, clothes go flying into the suitcase and more yelling: "Cash?" "Credit card—" "Which—" "Your Visa!" Paid up?" "Yeah—come on!" yells Stan, "If we forget something, tough! We'll buy it—let's get the hell— Bryce, can you drive? We're too freaked!"

You all pile into Peggy's '94 black Subie SVX and you're driving and you want to do what the speedometer says it can do—l6o but you're on the freeway, it's rush hour it's 35 to 40 mph but you get them there.

"Bro," says Stan, digging in his pockets, "extra set—your keys. We'll call."

And *bang*, inside the terminal—gone, swallowed up.

You drive back as if in a daze. Miserable traffic. Just like that. Snap of fingers. Things change. Chicago hit by tornadoes? You turn on the news; it's and it's all on KING news. "Chicago raked by at least two F-4 tornadoes, three smaller ones, still under tornado watch—excuse me—a new one on the ground, downtown—extensive damage."

You exit to 50th. Your head is spinning. It's around seven and you haven't eaten and somehow, you just aren't hungry. You pull into the driveway, grab the keys and it takes a few minutes to get the locks—part of the problem is that your hand is shaking. Finally you figure out which key opens which lock and you step inside. For a moment, the darkness, the quiet of the place us unnerving. You want to set up the TV but you don't have a clue how to do it; you're used to your ten dollar, yard-sale Sony. You do remember you have your laptop and, yeah, on ABC on-line—yeah—you watch Chicago devoured by swirling, angry, roaring winds of black.

☠ 4.

So. There you are. Sorta moved in but so unsettled. You turn off the computer. It's just too grim. You find your cell phone, dial Peggy's number but hit voice mail and you leave a message. "Hey, Bryce here. Wondering how you're doin'. Call when you can. Take care." You sit there and you realize how shaken you feel. You can't help but remember the predictions of even worse and more severe storms as the summer ice in the Arctic unexpectedly vanished. You remember the stories that you heard not too long ago—about the foot of hail dumped in New Jersey and how they had to call out the snowplows—in June. To the eight inches of rain in one hour in Philadelphia—to the pictures of kids with five inch hailstones.

You go up to the main floor, get a beer and sit on the deck looking out over Seattle. *It's all about global warming,* you think, *what the fuck is in store for us? Just how bad is it going to get?* You heard something from someone saying that you only had to look at the early 2000's to see what was in store, and by 2014, it was obvious Al Gore was right when he said we only

27

had ten years to fix it in his film, *An Inconvenient Truth*. Then the loss of summer sea ice in the Arctic. *Yikes*, you think, *yikes*. But still, no one knows the future. You drink the beer. No one knows. Scientists working like crazy. Things can change. Maybe they will. But right now, you just really wish you could hear back from Peggy or Stan—you close your eyes. *God, you think, been doing a lot of that—has to be stress, spacing out on stuff. I need to sleep. Maybe just a nap.* On your way to the bedroom, you stop and give the TV one more chance—you study the instructions and for whatever reason, the directions seem clearer than they were before. "Oh, OK," you say, "huh—why didn't I see that before?" You plug in the cable here, this one there and find the remote—makes sense. You turn it on. Nothing. *Doesn't make sense*, you fume. *I did everything right.* You glance down. "D'oh," you say, "forgot to plug it in. How could I not see that?"

You plug it in. *Bink!* On it comes and you stare, mesmerized. Virtually every channel has something on about Chicago. You stare at the carnage; the highrises, sky- scrapers with windows blown out. You shake your head in disbelief. *Chicago had lousy weather*, you think, *hot weather but—tornadoes? Boy, talk about the 'Windy City'. Yow!*

"—highly unusual weather patterns," the reporter says as the camera continues to pan and then switch to shots of neighborhoods. "We came across one neighborhood," continues the reporter, "Stacy Ingram has the story. Stacy."

Stacy is a nice-looking lady with chocolate brown hair, dark eyes and she's wearing a North Face rain jacket and in spite of her on-air professional presence, she looks worried. She goes up to an older bespectacled gentleman in a white shirt. His hair is thinning and age spots are liberally scattered on his face like freckles. "This is Mr. Anklwertz who saw what happened. Sir, can you describe what you saw?"

The gentleman looks like the proverbial deer caught in the headlights; hard to say if it was the cameras that had him spooked or what he had seen. You watch in rapt fascination as he tries to speak in a raspy voice that becomes a little stronger, as if he comes back to reality by speaking on camera. He looks directly into the camera and then looks down as if almost totally overwhelmed to the point where he can't look anyone in the eyes. "Just sitting down to dinner we heard this thunder then a blast of light—it was—it was right overhead and then the sky just turned black and it was like the sky—" he shakes his head, trying to find the right words to describe something indescribable, "the sky just—just—just—came down—and the building shook and windows blew out—my wife, my wife Missy, we jumped under the dining room table and then we heard cracks and pops and snaps and a crash we knew—I guess we knew that our 140 year old elm was coming down—" he turned and behind him, a shot of cars smashed by the huge tree. "—had to have been a tornado—oh, my God—"

You mute the sound. It's too much but the panning continues of cars piled on top of one another, trees down, roofs peeled away—

You stare and slowly shake your head. Peggy and Stan are flying into that carnage. *How brave they are*, you think, *for even flying*. Who wants to fly anymore? You remember a story about a big plane, a big plane that dropped out of the sky mid-Atlantic. Until they found the black box everyone was wondering if it was severe weather that brought it down. You hope Stan and Peggy call soon. Unconsciously you go about closing windows, making sure doors are closed, it's like even here in Sunny Seattle, you want to shut the weather out. You can't trust it anymore. Even though it gets warm real fast in the townhouse, you don't want to open anything up. Be caught off guard. You know you're being silly—but—tornadoes in Chicago? Oh, my God! You sit down, turn the TV on to something banal. Then you begin to feel really kinda creepy; a real sense of anxiety and you find yourself suddenly exhausted. *Must be all the stress,* you think, *must be—so tired—just close my eyes*—TV blathering on about a mattress commercial—"Sleep Country USA"—suddenly so sleepy—

—you're on that nice bed in the commercial. You saw yourself just walk on through that big screen TV and you're on that nice, comfortable bed. There is a smell coming from it and it's intoxicating. In-toxic-ating—you ponder why you separate the words like that. When you look again, it has the same feel as that wonderful carpet in Stan's place and you take a deep breath of it—you feel a dizziness, and it isn't bad, just makes you feel light-headed—

—a dragonfly with wings of jade lands close by and you look at the face. It's your mother. "Hello dear," she says in a high-pitched voice. "It's been awhile."

"Years," you say. "Last time I saw you we were in Sacramento."

"Do you still judge me harshly?" she asks.

"Why shouldn't I? You ran off with some fucker."

"Ever think maybe your father was an asshole?"

"I loved my dad—at least he got me to college."

Industrial Carpet Drag

"So you could get a dead-end job in that cultural dust bin of Seattle?"

You raise your hand and smash your mother into smithereens, and horrified, you see dragonfly goo all over your hand and the goo begins to move, dissolving your hands, the bones showing through and there is no pain and you watch horrified, beyond words, beyond anything you've ever imagined and in some place you know you always wanted to do that to her. Your dad was perfect. He was swell. Had she just done what he told her to do—you look down, your hand, your lower arm up to the elbow is gone—

"Sleep Country USA—"

You look down again, your hand is fine. Something inches up the mattress. It's a larger dragonfly, now made out of metal with sharp spikes. It is encrusted with diamonds. You hear it say, "A little seduction along with some pain? Care to imbibe, my ungrateful son?"

You watch your hand lift. You don't want it to do that. You will your hand not to do that. You want to take your other hand and hold it down but looking over, you see a huge cougar sitting on your hand. The cougar stares at you. Its look is unfathomable and you might as well be looking into two blue-rimmed black pools of space. Blue space stuff spinning about two black holes that take you to where you cannot guess and your hand pulls up and then it's like a string snaps—your hand slams down on the dragonfly—

—-stars. Stars. Stars. Brilliant blasts of light and a pain as if your arm has been suddenly jammed in molten lava.

Dumbly you watch your arm turn to steel which becomes encrusted by a glittering wave of diamonds, moving up your arm. You look to the cougar but the cat is gone, replaced by an octopus with the face of your father inked onto it. Somehow, you hear your father's voice. It sounds like a voice that you would hear underwater. "Proud of me still. Had you wrapped around me in all sorts of ways and you're proud of me still. Never was around too much but when I was, I made sure that your mother couldn't do much—about me, about my impact. My, but I was clever."

You muster up the courage to say, "How did you do what you did?"

"Trade secrets. But a bunch of money, loyalty induction and guilt-tripping helped a lot. Great way of getting back at your mother."

You watch the octopus slowly slide up your arm. You don't know why or how it does this with no water around. And some part of you knows this is truly bizarre, this doesn't make sense. But—

"—Like you're in a dream and you can't get out—" comes the voice as if through water. "Not only like you are in a dream, but you're just plain stuck there."

"How'd I get—"

—you sneeze. Startled, you blink, look around. Your right hand is fine. Nothing on your left. You get up, and realize that you have to go to the bathroom. You shake your head and you wonder what the hell that dream was all about.

You come back to the kitchen and get a glass of water. Then two. Then three—it's as if something is removed from your head, like you can think again. You find yourself calmer and you open the door off the second floor to the balcony. Somehow your head seems to clear even more. Must be exhausted from all the stress. Just the way it's playing out. *Yeah,* you think, *yeah, it's OK. Just exhaustion. Maybe too much pollen*—it is June and God knows what pollen can do to you. You go back in, find more Moosedrool and sit outside and savor it. The sky is nine p.m. June lovely, the setting sun sets the skyline glowing, Mt. Rainier looms pink and grand. *Lucky to live here,* you think, *away from crappy weather like Chicago. They've had rotten weather before, heat waves. Nothing new. Really. Given all this stuff is about global warming is true, we still got plenty of time to do something. Al Gore said we had ten years—we still got*—you stop, do some math in your head. *Didn't he say that in 2003-2004? That means we only got*—you shrug. *Ooops. That was a few years back. Ah, we'll think of something. Scientists working with new NanoParticle Computation and Enhanced Artificial Intelligence. We'll beat this. Any day.* You sit, drink in the view. You want to go down and make your bed but you can't quite remember where you put the sheets. *In some box around here somewhere. Go through all this shit tomorrow.* Besides, you're tired. Really tired. Beer probably doesn't help much but it's good. After a while, you go inside, find some avocado dip and some corn chips. And discover you really are pretty hungry.

Brreep Breep. Your cell phone rattles on the coffee table.

"Hey, Bro," comes the voice.

"Stan, God, good to hear ya dude. How ya doin'?"

"Well, not so good, not so bad. Peggy's mom's house has some shingles torn off. Bad news is that there could be more tornadoes tonight, tomorrow— less chance but could still happen. Everyone's pretty blown away—" he laughs, "no pun intended." Pause. "Just a minute dude. It's Peggy."

"Hi," comes her voice. Usually it has a real liquid quality about it, stretches out the vowels so it sounds real sensual but tonight, right now, pretty clipped and— scared. "Hi," she says again, "hi-uh—how are you—"

"I'm fine. How about you?"

"Wow," she says, then after a pause. "Lots of damage. Like bombs gone off. We're staying for at least a few more days just to make sure Mom and Dad are going to be OK, right now, they're pretty shaken— everyone is. They didn't get the worst of it. House couple of doors down was just sucked off its foundation and no one's seen it since."

You swallow. "Geeze," is all you can say.

"Anyway, we'll stay in touch. Remember to air the house out, OK? Probably no big thing but breathing that chemical crap may not be real good."

"OK," you say.

"Use the Subie whenever you want. We're so glad you're there."

"Yeah," you say, "glad to be here. Will take the truck back tomorrow."

"Oh, wow," says Peggy, "totally forgot about that. Keep track of the receipts. Oh, here's Stan."

"Dude. Have all the beer you want; restock it with something you like, OK, Bro?"

"Thanks. You guys take it easy and stay in touch. Watch the weather."

"Will do. Weird, wild and wacky weather. Anyway, take care, OK?"

"You too."

"Will call tomorrow, when l have a better idea of what's going on."

Industrial Carpet Drag

"OK."

"Bye. Later."

You do as they ask, open up a few windows, the sliders off the balconies though you're a little uneasy doing that. Ain't your house and you'd feel awful if someone got in and given that, you go outside, make sure the Subie is locked up and you really want to put it in the garage but there is still a lot of crap in there to be moved in. Anyway, you lock up everything, double check the front door, don't open anything on the lower level and make sure all the locks are secured and you check 'em again. *Being paranoid*, you think, *but it ain't my house.* You even decide to leave the bathroom light on. "I hear that's the number one thing that scares off burglars. Light coming out from a bathroom." you remember someone saying.

Back on the main floor, you chide yourself for being so anxious—you stop. Anxious. Where does that come from? you wonder. Never had a problem with feeling so anxious. *Gotta be because this isn't my place and I'm afraid I might screw something up here. Gotta get over this. I live here now. I pay rent here. I can come and go as I please here. This is my play-ce*—you stop. *Play-ce. Play Space. Place.* Your mind is getting interesting with what it does to words. *Why am I more aware of that now?*

You go to the kitchen, get more avocado dip and chips, sit down on the couch, look around and admire your surroundings. Having that half-wall jutting out from the right side of the unit and having the double-sided fireplace and the built-in bookshelves—what a nice, nice touch, you muse. And you admire your good fortune. Oh, what luck! You then flip on the TV. Coverage of the weather carnage continues. Then the stuff about overwhelming temperatures in the South—triple digit and 90 percent humidity. Wow. Flash floods in Utah. Then a report of a tornado in London and wild weather in Siberia. But here, here in Seattle, you smile. Nothing's gonna happen here. You watch the cable news. Long range forecast great. No rain. Just wonderful, beautiful weather.

You finish your avocado dip, the chips. Watching the TV, cable news network, local, talking about the pooch that gave a child hope to deal with his cystic fibrosis and donations are welcome. You snort. *Let's not talk about the real news—why the kid has to get donations and why there isn't health coverage to handle that. Oh, well.* You glance to your watch. *Wow*, you think, *midnight!* Then you start sneezing. It passes. You shake your head then you stand, look outside. In the east, in a cloudless sky, a full moon rises. Then you just sigh, and muse, *Oh, man, what great weather. Move some more shit upstairs tomorrow, then go out to Green Lake.* You smile, sigh again and you just close your eyes as you think, *So comfortable—and just love the smell of this new couch—*

And then the fun begins—

☠5.

Crash! Boom! RumbleRumbleRumble. ─midnight. Lightning rips the sky and the thunder sounds like it's right overhead. You get up. *What the fuck?* Without thinking, you race around, closing windows, the sliders. The wind howls and suddenly it's a downpour.

You switch channels and you get the local weather from sweet little red-haired Samantha Sefern who seems to be looking a bit bewildered, like she just can't believe what she's saying: "—advised to take down anything that could fly away—sudden storm—tornado warnings for Portland and Vancouver, Washington."

You stare with incomprehension as the lightning rips across the sky, the rain pounds and the wind howls.

Suddenly, it's quiet. You look around again. It's ten p.m. The TV is off. In a perfectly cloudless sky, the moon is high above, shining white, serene. *Nightmare*, you think. *Nightmare. Fucking nightmare.* Something seeming so fucking real that you actually thought you closed windows and sliders.

I did—didn't –I? All still open. You sit. You are aware that you are rocking. You stop. You think back. *When did I have all this weird crap begin to happen?* You begin to realize that it began happening when you started spending more time here. You dismiss it. Just not possible that stuff like rugs, paint, sealants, glues—no, it has to be stress. Just need more sleep.

You curl up on the sofa again. You've always loved the smell of new carpets and new furniture. It's as intoxicating as that New Car Smell. And the pillows. Those blue and red pillows—so comfortable. You admire Peggy's aesthetics.

Breep. Breep. The cell phone rattles on the table. "Hello?"

"Hi. This is MaryAnne."

"MaryAnne—oh, hi—how are—" *Oh, fucking shit!* You think. *I was supposed to meet her at Andy's for a drink at nine—* "Oh, my God," you say. "Ooh, my God. I am so sorry—I've helped a friend move into a place, tornadoes hit Chicago where Peggy's parents live, they took off—"

On the other end, a long pause. And in the voice, disbelief, "Are you jacking me around? Are you kidding?"

"No—I've been exhausted with all of this and I just plain—spaced—"

Long pause on the other end again. "You're serious."

"Serious." You think fast. "Where are you?"

"Home."

You flip on the TV and sure enough, CNN is still playing the footage of the carnage. "Look at CNN."

Rattle. Phone set down. Then in the background you can hear, "—two more tornadoes touched down later this evening, one on the south side, another weaker one near the lake shore. So far nineteen people killed in this unprecedented severe weather—"

"Oh, wow," says MaryAnne, "and your friends went in to that—?"

"Take care of Peggy's parents. Yeah."

"OK, I forgive you. Wow. I just can't believe—" pause "—can't believe it—"

"So anyway I'm at my new place where I've been all evening—guess it's sort of a townhouse—"

"Hey," says MaryAnne, "if that's the big surprise you've been hinting at, you just blew it."

Ah, crap! You think. *Damn. I was going to have her over and surprise her. Damn, I blew it.*

"And if it is that, well, how cool is that? And don't worry. Instead of being surprised, I'll be delighted for you and want to see it."

"Well, um, thanks. It really is an awesome place. Didn't even know I was going to be living here until a week or so ago when out of the blue, Stan offered a room for me at half the price and a billion times the coolness."

MaryAnne laughs. In that laugh, you hear that liquid quality of warmth that you hear in Peggy's voice. She continues to laugh. "Well, I can't imagine any downside to that. View?"

"Killer. He got it from a family deal—pays less in mortgage than I was paying for rent. Boy—wish I'd bought."

"Couldn't know," says MaryAnne. "So when are we going get together to connect and celebrate?"

"Your call," you say. "Your convenience, since I messed up."

"Talk tomorrow?" she asks.

"Yeah. This time, I call you. But hey, one question before you go—"

Pause on the other end.

"Um—this may sound strange—you know about any effects from outgassing of paint, carpets—"

"Huh—" she says. "—um—I've heard reports of people going bonkers but I think a lot of that's crap. I've got new carpeting and been fine."

"Hm," you say. "I kinda thought that. Just wondered."

"Talk to you tomorrow," she says.

"OK."

You're glad she gave her opinion. You want to believe it. You really do. You really, REALLY do. Then, a sudden panic—if it isn't outgassing causing this—stress, you think, *has to be stress.* You want to believe that—as much as you want to believe MaryAnne.

☠6.

You sit back down, and you think, *Wow. I don't want to blow it with MaryAnne, damn!* You know how attracted to her you are but also a little wary. She's a counselor, a therapist, loves the out of doors, loves cooking, loves life and she has an energy, a presence that you find very attractive—it's kind of unfamiliar—you ponder for a moment, *that means not of the family, doesn't it?* Learned that from MaryAnne when you two were out walking across Capitol Hill not long ago, walking past those stately mansions on 16th that Saturday, that early May morning with the air so cool and remember clearly both you walking and talking. You go up to Union and 20th to a ridge, an ancient glacial lateral moraine that included the valley that eventually became Lake Washington some two miles away and then beyond that to the opposite shore. You stop on that ridge and she says, "My favorite place; I love to walk by here every morning and on clear days, the view of the Cascades is so amazing." You look. She's right. It *is* amazing. The mountains, still snow-covered, are a vertical blue-white wall of some five to six-thousand feet.

Bruce Taylor

She continues. "Lot of people look at the Cascades and don't think they're high—point to the Rockies, to the 14,000-footers but you have to remember, it's all relative. If Seattle were the same elevation as Denver, the Cascades would be higher than the Rockies. Mt. Rainier would be—" she appears to think for a moment, "14,410 plus 5280—well, that's 19,690 feet—"

You look again at the Cascades. Suddenly, they seem a lot bigger. You both continue on, over to 35th and walk along what MaryAnne calls "Mansion Row"—houses on another lateral moraine that drops steeply away to the glacial scored gash that is the keep of Lake Washington. And you ponder at the money that it must have taken to have houses built resembling plantation houses out of Georgia or Virginia. You stop and just stare at one vast red brick edifice with a commanding view of the lake, and the Cascades from Baker to Rainier and then to Bellevue on the other side. You just stare. "Holy catz," you remember saying, "What would that be worth now?"

MaryAnne shakes her head. "Five million?" Her green eyes drink in the scene. She's wearing a brown sweater with blue highlights, a wide cloth belt with a simple knot in the front and blue jeans and blue turtleneck and right then you somehow really see her and begin to realize that she's a pretty nice lady but still something hangs you up. You know what it is. You don't want to look. But you're going to have to. You know that.

You continue on, on that bright sunny morning, marveling at the views, the houses of Mansion Row. You stop at the HiSpot Café, have lunch, and she surprises you—she treats. She's full of surprises like that. Attractive, but so, so unfamiliar. Over your artichoke omelet and her salmon omelet you chat. Light stuff. Getting-to-know you stuff.

"So how long you been in Seattle?" she asks.

"Fourteen years. Moved here from Sacramento in 2000. Moved here with Stan when I was eighteen to go to school. We were both accepted at the U."

She smiles. "Born and raised here. Traveled a lot, been to Europe, hiked in the Andes—but whenever I come back here—" She just shakes her head, that beautiful dark hair moves like a gentle curtain. "Beautiful," she says, "beautiful." She smiles. "Then I got a job at Harborview as a research assistant in the clinical psych department."

"Like it?" you ask.

"Strange," she says. "All psychiatry is medicine now. Talk therapy, the Id, Jung, Adler—all seen as quaint, that, in the end, it's just chemistry so you find the right chemicals, put them in a pill and presto, it's Brave New World: better living through chemistry." She shakes her head, takes a bite of her omelet and a sip of coffee. "Wow," she says, "great coffee."

You take a sip. "Yeah, it is. It really, really is."

"And you can kinda see where they are coming from—" she says, "you know, chemistry. Most people, for example, can't get access to insight until they are in their early thirties—the growth hormones are so powerful that they chemically block insight—so if you come from a dysfunctional background, when the growth hormones come into play at puberty, they act as a 'lid' to prevent deep insight because the body is all set for reproduction until the early thirties, then, as the growth hormones decline, you start getting insight, usually through dreams—"

You listen, totally blown away by what she says

because you have had some strange dreams. "That—that's really something—" you manage to say. "Have you—"

"Ohhhh, yeah," she says. "Ohhhh, yeah. There's a lot to that. Dreams about my father—and you?"

This is abruptly getting unsettling but she's being gutsy—

She grins and laughs. "It's OK. Probably about your mother."

You swallow. Boy, that's one hard piece of omelet you're swallowing. Man. How the hell could she know? You think back, Yeah, it was just after you turned 32 that the dreams began—that was March. You get brave. She's being brave and you say—

—*KA-BLAM! FLASHFLASH! KA-BLAM!* Your eyes fly open. You are totally disoriented. You look around. The TV is still on. *Where the hell was I? What the*—you look out and the sky is alive with lightning and thunder *BOOMS* and shakes the place. You scramble to your feet and run around shutting windows and closing sliders and thinking, *WHAT THE FUCK WHAT THE FUCK WHAT THE FUCK WHERE THE FUCK IS THIS COMING FROM IT'S NOT SUPPOSED TO DO THIS WHAT THE FUCK WHAT THE FUCK!* Then you catch yourself. *Wait a minute. This just happened. I was asleep. I dreamed this. This must be—FLASHFLASHFLASH—KA-BLAM—KABLAM—it's not—it's real how the fuck—?*

You flip to the local news and there's Geoff Runner, the weather forecaster for CableNews5 and a crawl in red at the bottom that reads: SEVERE WEATHER ALERT—SEVERE WEATHER ALERT: SEATTLE, TACOMA, WESTERN WASHINGTON—UNANTICIPATED SEVERE WEATHER MOVING IN

Industrial Carpet Drag

EXPECT LIGHTNING LARGE HAIL POTENTIALLY DAMAGING WINDS STAY INSIDE. And Geoff Runner is saying, "—a bit surprising about this wild and wacky weather but this is spring and this can happen. So batten down the hatches, it's going to be a stormy evening. So far in the last half-hour we've had 500 lightning strikes over the greater Seattle area. Whidbey Island Naval Air Station is digging out from five inches of hail, some as large as golf balls, damaging windshields and denting cars. Oh," and he chuckles as if he's talking about the price of watermelons, "wouldn't wanna be up there—might get clonked on the noggin—"

Gail Shenan, a cute little pixie of an anchorwoman laughs to put a light touch on it. "Well, Geoff, we just had some calls with folks wondering if all this wicked weather across the US is related to global warming and the loss of ice in the Arctic—"

Again, Geoff chuckles good-naturedly. "Oh, no no, no, this is just a little abnormality in the—" *FLASH FLASH FLASH KA-POW KA-POW ROAR RUMBLE—*"—stream and it's not really all that—" *FLASH-POW KA BLOOIE—fwizzt—*the lights go out and so does the TV. But it sure as hell isn't dark. You look out to see the sky just alive with fire, as jagged bolts of lightning flash across the sky like white-hot dendrites looking for connection. You stare in dumb shock. You've never, ever seen anything like that. Never. And you've seen a lot of shit, but never, EVER ANYTHING like THIS. You experience the sudden urge to crap.

—*pop-pip*—the lights come back as does the TV. You're now looking at a commercial showing three cartoon raccoons playing with toilet paper and

45

extolling its softness and goodness and how this toilet paper doesn't shred and stick to your butt. *Whew*, you think, *sure am glad we got our priorities right. Buying and selling shit just has to go on doesn't it?*

Tap. Tap. Bang. Bangbangbang! WHACK! WHACKA-BANGABANGA-BLAM!

You swallow. You look out to the deck. Hail. Hail as big as—fucking golf balls. And the place sounds like you're in a barrel with someone firing buckshot at it. *CLATTERCLATTER-ROAR—oh my God, Peggy's Subie*—you race down stairs—*what is that—*

Whoooooo!

FUCK!

WHOOOOOROAAARRRROOOOOO—

CLATTERCLATTER-RATTLERATTLE BANG-BANGBANG

SNAPCRACKLE-POP–CRUNCH! THUD! And the whole place shakes, shudders—then—it's eerily quiet. You go to the door and slowly open it. In the driveway floodlights, Peggy's Subie, with a poplar across the middle of it, looks like a weird black sausage squeezed in the middle. The front end is a good two feet off the ground and the hood has been dented and dinged by the hail. Further beyond, the rental truck's windshield has been busted out; branches sticking out from heaps of hail litter the driveway.

Cautiously, other doors open from the townhomes nearby and you can hear low, hushed voices, "—hear a tornado touched down—"

"No, it was a downdraft, Seattle doesn't get tornadoes—"

"We're not supposed to get golf-ball sized hail either."

Industrial Carpet Drag

Someone else calls over, "You folks OK? We lost our front window."

A fellow in a white bathrobe over pants comes out from the townhome next to yours, looks to you. "You OK?"

You gulp "Yeah-yeah—wow." You point. "So much for my friend's Subie."

The guy laughs. Points to a car with a tree across the hood, all the windows smashed. "So much for my Mercedes."

You go inside. *Should have parked the car in the garage but how the fuck was I to know what the hell am I going to tell Peggy oh, shit oh shit oh shit. God damn it. This wasn't supposed to happen.*

Back upstairs you hear, *Breeep Breep Breep.* The cell is almost rattling off the table.

Geoff Runner is still babbling on the TV "—reports of small hail and maybe even a small funnel cloud north of the ship canal but the winds were a little surprising—sixty miles an hour in some of those showers. But it looks like this wacky weather will be ending—"

You pick up the phone.

"Yo, this is Stan—we couldn't sleep and were watching the news—you guys got an F-2 tornado out there? Are you kidding?"

"—uh, yo, Bro—did you say F-2?"

"Yeah—"

"I just heard a small funnel cloud may have formed."

"We heard F-2 and that you got clobbered by hail and winds up to eighty—"

"Wow," you say, "sounds like you get better news there than we get here."

"Things OK?"

"No."

"What?"

"Lotsa damage. We may have been real close to that little funnel cloud that may have formed, according to the TV station here."

You hear the anxiety in Stan's voice—"—my house—"

"Can't tell," you say. "No windows busted—but the Subie—shish-ka-bobbed by a tree."

"DUDE! WHY DIDN'T YOU PARK IT IN THE GARAGE? GOD DAMN!"

'THERE WAS NO FUCKING ROOM IN THE GODDAM GARAGE—"

"WHY DIDN'T YOU FUCKING MAKE ROOM—!"

"BECAUSE NO ONE WAS FUCKING EXPECTING A GODDAMN TORNADO! WE DON'T GET FUCKING TORNADOES IN SEATTLE GOD DAMMIT IT WAS SUPPOSED TO BE FINE NO ONE SAID A FUCKING WORD ABOUT ROTTEN WEATHER YOU KNOW THAT LIKE I KNOW THAT SO FUCKING GET OFF MY CASE I'M FUCKING SORRY—"

Long silence on the other end. Real long silence. Really *really* long silence.

"—Stan—?"

"—yeah—"

"—if I'd known that there was a even a chance of a pigeon flying over and pooping on the Subie, I would have done everything to not have that happen—but there was nothin' in the forecast—no one knew— totally unpredicted—"

Long silence. Then. "Yeah. I know. I know. And I'm sorry—it's just a fuckin' car, for Chrissake but it's

Industrial Carpet Drag

Peggy's dream mobile—I—oh, what the fuck am I gonna tell Peggy? What the—" (muffled voice) "—Peggy wants to talk with you."

"—Bryce?"

"Yeah."

"You OK?"

You want to cry. "No."

"What?"

"Your car. I fucked up. I should have put it in the garage. I fuck—"

An angelic voice comes back. "Hey," she says, "Hey, hey—yeah it hurts, but no one—it's like here in Chicago—no one was expecting—" a long pause. "—anything like this—we heard what happened and it's the same thing—" Her voice tries to convey reassurance but you can tell how totally fucking stressed she is; the fear, the anger, the sadness. "You should have seen what it was like coming here," she continues. "The turbulence was incredible. Everyone on the plane was barfing or freaking out or crying. It was awful. We're going to try to come back by train or rent a car or something—we sure as hell are NOT flying back. There is just no way we are going to do that."

"How are your folks?" you ask.

"Pretty shaken. The tornado passed real close by and they have lots of damage—the roof, trees down all over. It's going to take a few days just to make sure they are going to be OK. We'll be in touch."

"OK. Thanks Peggy."

"Hey. Hey—don't worry about the car. Awright?"

"OK. Thanks."

"Be in touch. Bye."

"Bye."

49

Bruce Taylor

You close the phone, toss it on the coffee table. You go around the place; thankfully no damage that you can see but you really don't want to see how it's going to look in daylight. You make sure all the windows are closed, then you go out to the balcony. It's 11:30. You look up. The sky has cleared. The moon is shining brightly and it's as if—as if nothing has happened. At all.

☠7.

What a night, you think, *what a fucking night. Weird dreams, fucked up weather.*

Breep Breep. You pick up the phone. MaryAnne.

"Hi," she says and you can hear the worry in her voice. "I'm so scared. I was asleep and the thunder and hail just jolted me out of bed. I've never seen anything like it. You OK?"

"Oh, man—" you say, "oh, man—I've been having weird dreams and then this crap hits—place is OK but my friend's girlfriend—Peggy—her Subie looks like a squashed sausage. Scary—I think the tornado must have passed close by—heard this weird sound—like a wind but scarier—like a wind on steroids—"

"I just heard it confirmed as an F-2 and there may have been another one near Sea-Tac airport."

You laugh. "Ever heard of Gabriel Garcia Marquez?"

A pause. "Oh, yes, yes," she says, "wrote *A Hundred Years of Solitude* and several more—"

"Yeah, wrote one called, *Love in the Time of Cholera.* Maybe it's time for someone to write a sequel. *Love in the Time of Climate Decay.*"

She laughs but you can tell it's forced. *She's stressed,* you think.

"Probably sell well," she finally says. "I don't think I've ever seen so many potentially bad things happening at once."

You sigh. You don't want to go there, not now. More bad stuff you just can't handle and yet—"Yeah," you say, "yeah. Looks like that. Like the Earth is a house afire and where do you aim the fire hose." You laugh. "I'd invite you over for company—"

"I'd take you up on it, but a lot of the streets around here are a mess with trees down and limbs all over the place. Lights are out across the street but we're OK."

You remember walking by her place, over on Yesler and 20th—a huge sprawling complex—what was it—Central Park East or something like that—built in the early 80's when land was cheap and no one thought home prices would skyrocket though it should have been obvious that it would—she showed it to you on that day in May when you met at the coffee place kitty corner to the condo then hiked to HiSpot Café—

"Bryce?"

"Here—sorry—really tired and keep flaking off—mind wandering I dunno why—I think I'm ju-ssssst shhh-haken—"

Pause. "You almost sound a little drunk—" she says. "Slurred speech."

"Maybe getting drunk isss not a bad idea—" you say. "I must—must be really wiped out—movvvv—vved today—"

"Hey —get some sleep. Just wanted to check and guess I needed to have some reassurance—"

Industrial Carpet Drag

You are suddenly overwhelmed by a profound lethargy. "Wow—" you say, "just—so—so tired—"

"Stress," she says. "You been through a lot."

"All of us," you say.

"How about we talk tomorrow. Things will be calmer then."

"Yeah," you say. So tired. "We could talk tomorrow.

"—uh—we just kinda said we would—"

You shake your head. *Wow*, you think, *what is going on.* "I'm sorry. I have to get some sleep."

"OK. Take care."

"You doo—too, I mean."

You hit the call-off button. Lay back in the sofa—*can't think*—you think—*just can't concentrate—like brain is in a fucking fog. Be good to talk to MaryAnne*—you blank. *Tomorrow. Tomorrow? We said tomorrow, right? So tired. Want to sleep. Afraid to sleep.* Decide to channel surf and to your delight, it's the beginning of *Star Trek: The Next Generation.* And it's an episode you've seen before, "The Crystal Avatar," about a being that destroys planets. One of the crewmembers aboard the *Enterprise* had a son who was a researcher on a world that was destroyed by the creature. She's assigned the task to discover more about the creature, but only after she makes it clear that she harbors no ill will toward the entity. They soon discover that the entity is intelligent, and that it destroys worlds not to be nasty but because the planets are food. The researcher discovers the frequency by which the creature communicates. The creature responds, comes near the starship for maybe some friendly interspecies dialogue, and the researcher abruptly amps the frequency, destroying the creature in what she feels is justice for the death of her son.

You watch that. Great effects, great program and MaryAnne likes *Star Trek* too and it's as if the boundaries to the plasma HD TV fade, fade, fade away and you look around and you are on a starship like the Enterprise, but not like it, and sitting next to you is MaryAnne. You don't question why you are there; it's like a dream and you are in orbit around a planet that looks like Earth and you are in a suit that resembles a Federation Starship Uniform but isn't—it's deep blue with a red, diagonal slash across the chest signifying some rank of which you cannot fathom. MaryAnne is in a magenta uniform with a yellow slash across her chest meaning something but it doesn't matter but what you are saying does matter as you look at the planet and she says, "Captain Bryce, we have been all over the galaxy. We have found that other civilizations do not exist. Voyager has led us nowhere. It really is all science fiction. And the only fact we know for absolute certain is that Earth exists and until we know otherwise, it is all we have. It is all there is."

"Indeed," you say, "indeed, it is all we have."

"What if," she begins, "what if Lovelock was right and the Earth is intelligent and all species of Earth, including us, are manifestations of that intelligence?"

"It's a game changer," you say. "We'd have to start over. If we don't—"

She nods. She turns to you with those green eyes, green, the color of life, of growing things, it is as if life itself is looking at you, maybe she, maybe all women, as the carriers and creators of life, are the Spirit of Gaia, looking at you and she says, "No matter what,

Industrial Carpet Drag

Earth, and the Spirit of Gaia, will prevail, with us or without us—Earth will prevail."

A thought. Earth as Gaia or the Crystal Avatar—but the revenge? Born of the planet, of Gaia, yet cursed with our knowledge of mortality, out of the rage at knowing this, we seek revenge, we destroy?

You look at MaryAnne; you close your eyes and when you open them again, you are in a bed, looking out of a skylight at eye level and you see Mount Rainier in the distance. "Beautiful, isn't it?" she asks.

"Yes. We must be in your condo—this is the loft you told me about."

She smiles.

You're under covers and she nestles close to you. Is this real? Are you so in-toxi-cated—that word again. *Why do I fixate on that word?* you wonder. *What does it really mean? I'm toxic? I am toxic or I've been exposed to something toxic and am under the influence. In-toxi-cated.* Usually refers to alcohol. You imagine you can access a print dictionary; you imagine you are running your finger down the page of the second volume of *Webster's Third New International Dictionary and Seven Language Dictionary. Yes: from intoxicare, French for— poison. I'm being poisoned? How? From what?*

As if reading your mind, MaryAnne says, "It isn't necessarily a bad thing, in-toxi-cation. Remember the Roman saying, 'in vino veritas'?"

You think for a minute. "In wine, truth?"

"Maybe whatever we experience is all right if we just learn to ask the right questions."

"What can possibly be OK about disease? Or cancer? What about Global Warming?"

She kisses you. "Maybe the answer to the first two

questions is that's the way the body experiences stress. You know that only ten percent of the population never gets sick? Nothing ever happens to them, and they die of old age."

"Genetic?"

"Maybe joy," she responds. "Global warming?" she continues.

"Too much carbon dioxide."

"Maybe it's overpopulation,"

You get it. You have to ask the right question.

"You just turned 32," she says. "Your dreams?"

You feel a sudden anxiety. A thought flashes in your brain: Dreams may be messages. The back door to insight. You look at her. She is ageless. She has knowledge beyond knowledge. And you know she knows her stuff and because she knows her stuff, she can easily guess your stuff.

"You're lovable," she says.

No, I'm not, says another part of you.

"I heard that," MaryAnne says. "Are you going to run from love or are you going to stay and learn the truth—that you're lovable? Or are you going to try to prove that part of you that lies—speaks the truth—by running from me?"

You don't know what to say. You sense you are indeed in-toxi-cated, in a toxic state, in-poison-ated. It's horrific because you feel the doors opening, the doors opening to fear, the fear –the fear—it's always the fear—

You jolt yourself awake. What—what—suddenly, you feel cheated. On the brink of something, some knowledge but held back, jolted back to the here and now. You look around. You rub your eyes. So close to something. Maybe not in-toxic-ated enough. You look

Industrial Carpet Drag

at your watch. 1:00 a.m. You rub your eyes again. That feeling of being cheated—wanting something but fearful of it. Fearful. Fearful of—what?

The TV is still on. It's a commercial for Amblnex, for anxiety. Right question, wrong answer. Feelings are meaningless, medicate them if they get too pesky. *Live in a state of chronic euphoria,* you think. Never mind that it's as stupid and nuts as always feeling depressed or whatever else.

Restless. Restless. You go downstairs. Feeling woozy but oh, that new carpet smell is like a perfume, mingling with that fresh paint smell and somehow that's soothing, almost—amozzzzt in-toxic-ating—you stop. What were you just about to do, anyway? For whatever reason, maybe to bring you back to a sense of reality, whatever that is, you want to go outside, see the damage and maybe figure out what to do. You open the front door. The Subie SVX sits in the driveway, in the moonlight, shiny and beautiful, showroom new.

☠8.

You come back upstairs, and you sit and you shake. You hold yourself. You don't know what to think. You switch to the weather channel. Pictures of a tornado-ravaged Chicago, you assume. "—and clean-up efforts continue in this tornado-flattened city. Confirmed 5 tornadoes this last evening. Two F-5's. That's two F-5's. Known dead, 24 people, three people died when baseball-sized hail smashed windows at a hospital. Looks like more tornadoes could happen tomorrow and Chicago remains under that threat as well as Cincinnati, Detroit, Cleveland. In the next several days, as these storms move east, New York, Washington D.C., and New England are all going to see severe weather with the real potential of tornadoes." The camera focuses away from the chaos and back to a weatherman in a dark suit, red tie. His black hair is short and he looks like he's in his twenties. "In other related news, it's triple digits in the South, with humidity at 90 percent and the heat-related deaths are mounting from those not able to get to cooling centers in time. Torrential rains, up to a foot an hour have wiped out rail lines in North Dakota. Flash flood alerts remain posted all through northern Arizona and into Utah." The fellow laughs. "Who would have thought that the best weather you're going to find is on the west coast, clear up to Portland and Seattle. The good weather just continues—"

You pick up the cell phone and look at the calls that have come in. Stan at 7:13 pm, MaryAnne at 9:36. That's it.

You can't believe it. You just cannot believe it. You go back downstairs. You open the door, you go outside and you walk up to the Subie. Perfect. Not a scratch. Not a ding. No tree limbs. Dry pavement. No broken glass from the rental truck. And you notice something else. Just being outside, you feel calmed, like your head is clearing. Instead of feeling so freaked out, you find yourself saying, "The right question." And for some strange reason, for some strange reason—   .

—you head back upstairs. *I must be so stressed by what is going on with Chicago—I'm having nightmares. That must be what this is all about.* In spite of this, you still feel better with the TV on. Maybe what you are learning is how you handle stress? Is that what is coming up for you at this magic age?

You curl up on the couch. Is that really possible? Is that really right? That you just can't have insight— real insight—until later? Are we that bio-chemically determined? Our Fate so cast by hormones? Oh, that couch, that new—furniture smell and you feel a little lightheaded and you close your eyes—

—walking across the sands of some planet with

Bruce Taylor

MaryAnne under a pale green sky. With two moons looming large above the horizon. "I know," says MaryAnne, "I know, I know. It's right out of *Forbidden Planet* and yes it looks like Altair 4, and for its time, the movie showed the true power of science fiction and what it was capable of doing and how it held itself back from being so powerful. But besides that—" she stops, picks up a molded piece of metal. "Huh," she says, "something from the Krell." She drops it in the sand and continues on. "The message of the film is more important today than it ever was—'Beware! Monsters from the Id.' You've heard that, right?"

"Who hasn't?" you laugh. "It's a cliché, almost a joke and it would be funny if it weren't something that we needed to take so seriously." You scuff along in the sand, vaguely noticing that your uniform as well as MaryAnne's, are like those that the crew wore on the ship, only instead of grey, they are, for you, sage green; for her, brick red. The colors probably mean something but you cannot fathom what that might be. You continue. "Not a lot different really than what Plato said, 'The unexamined life is not worth living.' Or, Erasmus, in 1514: 'The worst of madness is to learn what has to be unlearned'."

You both begin climbing up a long, sloping hill and, as you reach the top, abruptly it becomes dark. From this vantage point, and looking back, you can see the members of the rescue ship firing on the Id-monster, its outline in fiery red from the state of the art special effects at 1956 Disney Studios.

"It's a little fakey," you remark, after a minute, "especially the guns, firing the, I guess, laser blasts—but for 1956—not bad." You nod in appreciation.

Industrial Carpet Drag

"Special effects that couldn't be touched until 1968—12 years later, with *2001, A Space Odyssey*." You shrug. "Just have to appreciate the artistry there."

You and MaryAnne watch the battle continue. "Extraordinary concept," MaryAnne says. "Still extraordinary. How much power the Id—or Unconscious—really has. And unless we acknowledge it, examine it and ultimately embrace it—"

"We're fucked," you say.

"And we may well be, as you say, fucked. Because this is something that we don't readily do. If we did—if we did—if we, as a culture, truly embraced and looked into the nature of our motives—there would be no wars, no hunger, no global warming—because everyone would be treating each other the way they, themselves, would want to be treated."

You admire the look she has, lips firm in conviction, looking straight ahead, to the scene before you, to the hope beyond. It's a heroic look and you like that. "I like what you say," you begin. "I'm afraid right now empathy is in rather short supply."

She nods. "Oh, I know," she says, "I know. And it's heartbreaking to see the disparity between what we could truly be—and where we are—in reality."

You both look at the scene below you. The Monster from the Id fades away. You know the next scene—the confrontation of Dr. Morbius as he grapples with the idea that the monster is his own Id, powered by the Krell technology harnessing the energy of the core of the planet, coming after him and what he must do—to embrace it.

"Such a clear lesson," you say, "know thyself. The truth shall set you free."

Under the two moons and that alien sky,

MaryAnne turns to you. "What is your Id-monster that you must you embrace?" she says.

Suddenly panicked, you wake up, turn on the couch, catch a commercial for Viagra. The boundaries of the plasma screen vanish. You find yourself sitting with the couple in the commercial. The fellow is you, the woman—the woman is the lady who left for New York. Though you are with them, they do not see the you of the present; rather they see the you at that past time.

Lana is twenty-eight, you, 30. Lana is Asian, dark-eyed, sensual, quiet—except When She Has Something To Say. And boy, does SHE have something to say. "I have to go to New York." she says, "You live in a dingy apartment and you aren't real happy in your job—I got things I want to do. What about you?"

You don't quite know what to say. But one thing that comes to your mind—why does this sound so familiar?

Oh, yeah, your mom saying to your dad, "You aren't happy, you don't do anything. You're depressed and I deserve better and so does Bryce."

Your dad stands up for himself in the only way he can—badly. Whining. "If you'd just get off my back, things will get better." He's a weasely kind of guy who you always thought the world of—until now. He turns into a large, necktie-wearing mosquito buzzing around, trying to take what he can get and—not giving much back. He comes after your mother. She's a big lady, and up until now, passive, but now it's different. She swats him away.

"Shoo," she says, "shoo. Go 'way." She bats at him with a white umbrella that, when opened, has the outline of a spider done in black thread.

Industrial Carpet Drag

Your father whines a little more then—buzzes off.

You liked your dad. He was always nice to you. He always confided in you and he was your buddy. But—*Oh*, you think, *oh—he never took much interest in me—did he? He was interested in me only if I was there—for him.* You look around for your mother but she's gone. She split. You ended up with your grandmother who didn't care much for kids and a grandfather who had some marbles rolling in the wrong direction, though he did take you out hiking and on the trail, he was different, like he somehow came alive. And that's about the *only* time you saw that. And they did get you to college 'cause they had the bucks and it was a way they could maybe absolve the collective guilt over being lousy parents themselves. And then there's Lana—cute Lana. Multi-orgasmic Lana, good friend Lana who loved you—you thought, until she got tired of her growing when you weren't. Or didn't care to. Or want to. Satisfied with a dumpy apartment but not really satisfied with it. It did what it was meant to do. Not far from a job that you were satisfied with but not really satisfied with but it did what it was meant to do.

Never heard from Lana again. Or Fran or Melinda or—you add it up. What happened to all those good ladies anyway? Why is it you went to college, met a lot of people, graduated with honors and, so what?

What happened? Deeper. How does one come to know that which one must come to know?

You look around. No one there. The space is white and stays white. It's as if you are in a white box. You hear a buzzing and before long, a dragonfly appears. It's large, the size of a Shetland pony and there is a saddle on its back. The body is almost a metallic blue, the wings shimmer. You know what has to happen next. You climb on—

☠9.

You come awake long enough to shift position on the couch. You inhale that luscious smell of new furniture mixed with the other odors of new construction. Seems to get more potent because you closed the windows, the doors, and . . . you . . . and . . . time seems to go elsewhere—

—flying on the back of the dragonfly. Is it your mother? You feel guilty for killing her but—is she back? How—? Confusion. But you begin to see—you stop. Begin to see. How is it we begin to see? And as that thought comes to your mind, you pass through a thunderstorm of flashing broken glass shards raining around you and the smell of ozone is potent and the thunder doesn't *crash* or *boom* but goes *La-la–la-de-da* like a child's song.

Like in a dream that makes no sense but that's fine if it's asking the right question to get the right answer and it's assuming that it's okay the way you're going because maybe, just maybe, this is the way it's gotta be if you're sure you move with good intent.

—sky clears, now it's that pale green like Altair 4

but you aren't sure and you trust the dragonfly—you have to 'cause right now it's the way it is and something must be working 'cause Stan and Peggy want you there to be with them in that house, in their lives, so something worked somewhere or maybe they put up with you and saw you as somehow harmless and pathetic and were just feeling sorry for you—you're not sure which.

Right at that point, the dragonfly lands. All around you it's still white space, and you get it that wherever this is, it could sure use some color. The dragonfly moves in such a way that you slide off the saddle then in a blur of movement of wings, takes off, turns into a pale blue dot and vanishes in a sudden sunbeam and you are reminded of an image of Earth, that pale blue dot, caught in a sunbeam, photographed by a space probe and the name of a book by Carl Sagan. But that's neither here nor there and you turn around and there is a figure up ahead. You hurry after it and as you approach, you see the baggy, brown-drawered, stooped posture and it's Mr. Blaklavach, your former landlord. He turns to you, his face is that of a spider. "Don't be alarmed," he hisses, "it is but your reflection. Nothing more."

You stop.

"No, don't stop," hisses Mr. Blaklavach. "Walk with me and learn something." You walk, and a minute passes. "You don't think I know that you did not like me and that you would have loved to put rotten meat in the refrigerator for me to discover?"

You gulp.

"Passive aggressive little shmuck," says Mr. Blaklavach.

"Don't mean to be that way."

Industrial Carpet Drag

"Good start," says Mr. Blaklavach. "Now how about apologizing to me for blaming me for the position that you put yourself in by renting a place that you didn't really like from someone that you didn't really like."

You don't know what to say. This hits you in the face like a ball of shit.

"I bet this feels like you're being hit in the face by a ball of shit," says Mr. Blaklavach. "Because that's exactly what it is. No one ever cared enough about you to tell you some things about you, did they?"

"—um—guess not."

"Pity," hisses Mr. Blaklavach.

You walk a little while longer and you let this all this sink in.

"You letting this all sink in, Mr. Bryce?"

"—um—"

"Gods. I call you by the wrong name and you don't even correct me. You are a mess. So were your parents. And your grandparents. Especially your mother's. And your great-grandparents. Don't you have anybody in your fucking family that has got *some* spine?"

"My mother?"

"Bitch," says Mr. Blaklavach. "Conceited bitch and your dad was a conceited self-absorbed prick. Match made in heaven or hell. Your choice."

"Wait a minute—" you say, turning, facing Mr. Blaklavach.

"Better," he says. One of his eyes vanishes. You get it. Seven more to go.

"I didn't choose what happened to me—I didn't want that stuff—"

"Specifics," says Blaklavach. "Specifics please. What stuff in particular didn't you want—"

"—um—all that dysfunction—"

"Nice try," says Blaklavach. "Fancy word. Means nothing. What stuff? Fear? Anger? Anybody who comes from a bad background where they didn't feel safe is sitting on all sorts of crap. What particular stuff do you mean?"

You can't answer.

"I know, you can't answer. It's OK. I'm not deliberately trying to upset you except that part of me is just showing you how much you don't know about you. I'm doing you a favor. Gonna thank me?"

"Thank you—I guess."

"So you're thanking me for walking all over you? Boy, what's wrong with you?"

In spite of this, you notice that one eye still has not come back.

"You probably think that in spite of all of this, you notice that one of my eyes has not come back. That's because your ignorance isn't exactly all your own. If you don't have a healthy model, it's hard to be healthy but I know you're trying and boy are you trying."

"Look—!" you say, "I can't know what I don't know but at least I'm still talking to you because if I didn't have something, you'd be doing something else with someone else so I'm here to learn something from you."

"Better," says Mr. Blaklavach. Another eye vanishes. Six to go. "So," he continues, "what did happen? I can guess but I want to hear it from you."

You've kinda gotten used to the eyes but you're glad they are disappearing.

"I bet you've gotten used to my eyes but I also bet you are glad they are disappearing."

You feel exasperated and a little naked. "How'd you know that? Maybe you're wrong."

Industrial Carpet Drag

"Picking up on your energy. Lots of what people say isn't through words. It's through the energy they give off. No one ever cared enough about you to tell you that, did they? So. You got idea zero about the impact you have on others."

"You can read me that well?"

"Yes, yes I can."

"How?"

"May sound funny coming from someone with what you think has some spiders in 'em, but it's the vibes. Another way of putting it—been around the block a few times. Built a lot of webs in my life, trapped more than one thing."

You find yourself regarding Mr. Blaklavach in a way you had never thought possible—with respect. He's up-front. You don't have to guess. And you like that.

"I bet you're beginning to like me," says Mr. Blaklavach. "because I don't play games and you don't have to guess and so forth and so on. Thanks. You're right." Another eye vanishes.

"The word," you say, "transparency?"

"Yes," says Mr. Blaklavach, "up to a point. Knowing when and who to be that way with and knowing whom you dare not be that way with. And along with that, always being transparent is as fruitcake as never being transparent. Political. Gotta be careful. Protect yourself."

Anguish erupts deep within your guts. The few minutes with Mr. Blaklavach energizes you as it depresses you. How much you didn't get of what you needed and didn't get. You begin to get it.

"Needless to say," begins Mr. Blaklavach.

"I know," you say. "You're right. I'm beginning to discover how much I didn't get."

You sneeze.

Mr. Blaklavch sighs. "Well, one thing you didn't have from me was a toxic waste dump."

"Huh?"

"That new place. New construction. Rugs, paint. Outgases crap like crazy—"

"Yeah," you say, "but not for—"

"Bullshit," says Mr. Blaklavach. "Part of what you are going through is not just related to your age— remember toxic crap pushes the hormone envelope—"

You stop looking at those five remaining eyes. "I was told outgassing was harmless."

"Of course. You think manufacturers would ever admit for one second what outgassing does to people? That it can cause memory loss, anxiety, depression numbness, slurred speech, in some cases seizures and can bring on Multiple Chemical Sensitivities? You want class action suits and manufactures to get sued?"

You sneeze again. Blood.

"I forgot to mention nosebleeds. Some reports of lung cancer. Hallucinations."

Happily, you notice the nosebleed stops.

"Did I mention some cancers?"

"No."

"What you are experiencing right now, with me— may be in part due to outgassing of paint, maybe the PCBs in the carpet, flame retardants in the sofa you're napping on—"

"I understand—" you say.

"But in a brain-fog, volatile-organic-compound-induced-sleep-way, I'd suspect. Until relatively recently," hisses Mr. Blaklavach, "rugs outgassed

Industrial Carpet Drag

formaldehyde. So even though you thought the place you rented from me was a dump—it was a toxic-free dump. You benefited. Nonetheless, maybe you should step out of this dream long enough to open a window. You still got a long night ahead."

For whatever reason, this discussion brings out a great respect for Mr. Blaklavach.

"Think nothing of it," says Mr. Blaklavach. Two more eyes vanish. Three to go. "And stop keeping track of my eyes. If you see me differently it's only because you see yourself differently. Right?"

"Guess so."

"Not guess so. Know so. Know as in conviction. *Sabe usted?*"

"*Da.*" You grin.

"*Nyet*-wit."

You feel genuine affection emanate from him; a gruff, rough affection. The frankness was intoxicating in the non-poison sense of the word.

"You're getting better," says Mr. Blaklavach. "Yes, I do like you after all."

One more eye vanishes. What remain look—pretty good.

☠10.

You come back to the here and now long enough to notice that your nose is wet. You rub it. Coagulating blood. Mr. Blaklavach. Open window. You stumble to the sliding door and open it. The coldness slaps you in the face. How can it possibly be so cold? It's June—it has to be in the 40's out there and you find yourself shivering. You compromise by closing the slider most of the way but for an inch or so. You look to your watch. 1:30 a.m. You're not sleeping real well and you kinda remember what Mr. Blaklavach was saying but you shake your head. You're healthy as a horse. Never been sick. Can't be this shit in the room. Crap. Must be the fucking pollen—you go the bathroom—but you can count on the fingers of one hand how many nosebleeds you had in your life and one of those was from being whacked in the face by a Frisbee. *Bad catch*, you think. You wash your face; glad it wasn't too messy and didn't go on long.

You stumble back to the couch and flop down and it's a CNN report on a fire raging in California—

"—unheard of," the announcer says breathlessly,

Industrial Carpet Drag

like maybe this is really cool video and exciting stuff for the insomniacs in the nation to stay sleepless some more as they present cool video and products to boot like Rogaine, sending in scrap gold for cash, hearing aids and snazzy wheelchairs from the Wheelchair Store "and Money Back Guarantee if you aren't satisfied and you get the chair free if Medicare won't reimburse you." (*Whatta deal*, you think, when you saw that ad earlier, *whatta deal. I can hardly wait.*)

—but anyway you watch the fire and you remember being down there in Orange County with Lana and her mom—

—you're in the car again in the back seat and you can see the temperature on the instrument panel on the dash and outside it's 117 degrees and Lana and her mom are talking—"—well personally," Lana is saying, "I think skin care products really make it with bosses because you gotta remember you're a face to the public and when you present the brownies and the Kool Aid to clients, they always appreciate it and slip a twenty between my boobs—"

You glance outside and you've gone from the deepest snows in the San Gabriel Mountains in recorded history, or at least the last thirty thousand years, to the snows abruptly melting turning everything around the freeway into an ocean.

"Well," says Lana's mom, thin, wiry with graying hair cut short. Looking out through blue, plastic framed glasses with little decorative raised penises in each corner, she says, "in my day, you had to put out a lot; you know, Martinis at noon, sex at one thirty and getting balled wasn't really so bad and the cumpensation was amazing." She slaps herself in the face in mock-anger. "Did I just make a bad pun? I think I

73

did. Dirty Dana! Dirty, dirty Dana. I am so dirty." And she laughs. "Boy the Dicks I've seen. And the Peters." And she laughs, "And the Peters. I know you've asked who your father was and it could have been anyone. You were an accident, but a nice one."

Lana turns into a dragon and scorches the interior of the car, then melts the glass in the window and the water outside has become thick with oil from numerous Exxon Valdez-type accidents everywhere you look and, of course, it ignites. Somehow the window replaces itself and Lana turns back into something that is halfway between human and dragon. From the rear seat, you can see a subtle scale pattern on her face, the long scales on her hands, the split pupil of the eyes but the hair remains the same. You touch it and realize it's made of the finest, thinnest glass you have ever felt. You look at the ends and see all the lights and realize it's fiber optics— bright little points of red, white, blue, green. Satisfied, you let her hair fall back. You look outside the window. Flames everywhere. Ahead, flames arch over the road, creating a bright and searing tunnel. The temperature is 250 degrees, remarkably cool for the fire you see. Things must not be really heating up yet.

"What about you?" Lana's mother says, glancing to you in the review mirror. "How big is your wad?"

"Big enough," says Lana. "He can go for hours. I just cum and cum and cum. I cum so often that I forget I cum. I start doing quadratic equations in my head while I sit there jerking and twitching in fucking delight. I said, fucking, fucking delight. I think I may also have discovered another aspect of string theory last time I came. Boy, where good sex takes you."

You blush. "Glad to be of service." You grin.

Industrial Carpet Drag

"Boy," Lana's mother says, "boy, I get wet just thinking about it."

Oh, you think, *oh, OK. That's what's heating things up.* The temperature is now 350 degrees and the whole world out there must be fucking burning and exploding in some sort of Gaia Sex or something. Through the smoke, you see a city engulfed in smoke. Might be Los Angeles, Salt Lake City—you really don't know where you are and the speedometer reaches 390 MPH. The freeway is totally clear in both directions and you are just zipping along, just scooting through those flames and the mother says, "Chicken. I just realized how good it would be to have baked chicken tonight. Don't know why I would have a desire for that."

Lana has become even more human-looking but the dragon eyes remain. "I guess chicken isn't my thing. Twinkies. I've always liked Twinkies. You know, they are filled with so much stuff that they can last years?"

"Hey," you say, "longevity. Eat enough Twinkies and you might live forever. Never thought of that."

Outside, the road ahead is melting. The temperature on the dash, 600 F. *Wow*, you think, *250 more degrees and it will be like we're driving on Venus. Wouldn't that be cool?*

You find yourself thinking about that, not so much driving on Venus, but the once Goddess of Love, the planet thereof, sure turned out to be a Sulfuric Acid Hell Hole. Is that it? You wonder. Behind all the funsy stuff and romantic stuff and Hollywood Stuff, that much of love is like the Hellhole Venus where you have to take a lot of heat to make something work and even then, something makes the landscape corrosive

75

and inhospitable. After all, if it were the other way, my mom and dad would still be together so maybe love is mostly a lot of heat and you have to endure the heat if you want to dance in the fierceness of Venus.

"—so I said to Susie," Lana is saying, "that I want to be a celebrity. That's what I want. And old pug-face in the back seat there, he just wants to wang me and be happy in a dumpy apartment and a dumpy job and watch *Star Trek* reruns. I want more. I want the stretch limos, the coke, the 24/7 in an afternoon. I want the good life. I want to see the biggest dicks in the world and fuck till dawn and get cum all over me, head to foot, dumped on with lots of sperm swimming all over me, licking my titties, humping their way up my cuntsy-wuntsy and yeah, they may get frustrated by the spermicide and the pill and the Dalkon Shield and the IUD but I ain't ready to get P-G—ya know?"

"Oh, my dear, dear daughter, you honor me and you flatter me. You're acting out my fantasies of freedom that I wish I had but I was stuck at GE just getting routinely fucked by corporate morons who couldn't see beyond their dicks. You want that and the Big Life, the *Life Magazine* life, the *National Enquirer* life—"

"That's right," Lana says, "that's right. Old Mr. Gray in the backseat, yeah, he's good in bed but in spite of how many times I shred his sheets, he thinks too small. Can't deal with that. Gotta move on. Gotta move on. Hey," she says to her mom, "we gotta bake some cookies tonight."

"Already thought of that, my TLC, my Tough Little Clit!"

From somewhere, she produces a tray of cookie dough and hands it to Lana who plops it in the glove compartment. A second later, there is a bright *ding!* sound and Lana pulls out the tray and passes the cookies over to her mother. In an off-hand way, she tosses several in the back seat, as if tossing them to her pet. You grab a cookie and it's warm, moist and just right like fucking Lana is warm moist and just right and you eat that cookie and see yourself fucking Warm and Moist and Just Right Lana and boy she eats it up and she'll never leave and you remember your daddy saying, "Fuck 'em right and they'll never leave." Maybe that's why he turned into a big, whining mosquito, so busy sucking and fucking that it never dawned on him that his wife, your mother, would leave. But she did.

Bigger and better things. Why does this sound so familiar? Why is Lana in your life?

The Warm-and-Moist-and-Just-Like-Lana-Cookie you eat, but you get it she ain't sticking around and outside now, the tires are smoking and the temperature on the gauge reads 850 degrees and you rejoice, you're on Venus! You're on Venus! Goddess of love! Yes!

And then Lana does something, She reaches beneath her seat and the roof over your head pulls back. Above you, the flames boil, roil and roll and Lana screams, "I'm off to New York, dumpy drawers! Hot sex ain't enough!"

And the seat becomes an ejection seat and you blast out of the car. You see the car turn into a fireball and you fly upward, upward through the roiling flames.

☠.11.

You realize it's hot and you know you aren't sleeping all that well. This is bad and the dreams and whatever else is going on is driving you nuts. You get up, open the slider a little more. Now it's hot outside. Whacko weather. Whacko, whacko weather. *Boy*, you think, *sure seemed like it was whacko here, boy what a dream. I need a sleeping pill*, but you realize you've never had to take them. Always slept well. You go into the half-bath on the second floor and there are some cardboard boxes in there, some smaller ones on the counter and some larger ones stacked on the floor. The labels on top and sides read: "Bathroom Stuff 1, Bathroom Stuff 2. Bthrm Stff 1/2—*funny*, you think, *they even abbreviated the half-bath. Funny.* You find yourself giggling as if it's the funniest thing you've ever seen at the same time thinking to yourself, *why the fuck is this funny?* as you paw through the boxes for something to help you sleep—Tyrptophan, something something something—*Huh? AMBLIFOR. Huh*, you think. *Huh. Over the counter stuff.* You scan the directions but your eyes are blurry from lack

78

Industrial Carpet Drag

of sleep and you read something about Pregnant Women, and Don't Take if You Are Taking something or other and blahblah. You need something; it's over the counter so it's harmless, probably some concoction of cookies, milk and Valium, who knows it's over the counter it's safe. You pop one and almost instantly you feel this warm soothiness coming over you like from some sort of calmness dust—*oh, my,* you think and you stumble toward the soft sofa—*oh, my, oh, my that's—oh, my*—that and that nice carpet smell and your mind goes pastel pink—

—Mr. Dinglepood sits there. He kinda looks like your kindly old grandfather on your mom's side who got hauled off for being too friendly to children. God, you never guessed he'd be that way. Such a kindly old fart, soft spoken, 70's, white hair, clean-shaven with a perpetual bulge in his pants that you never thought too much about. You were a kid. Maybe that's where he always carried his banana.

So anyway, Mr. Dinglepood is kinda looking like that: thin face, kind eyes, like you remember your grandfather had—a guy who also liked cats and especially liked to have his hands below their tails which some cats liked and others whirled and clawed the crap out of him. He'd just smile. Never did it to dogs. Couldn't get away with it, you guessed. Dogs are smart so maybe there was something to your grandpa being hauled away.

Mr. Dinglepood sits there in a rocker and you approach him in this pink world and he says, "I'm not even going to ask how or why you named me this," he says. "Probably says more about you than it does me. My name is—" he pauses, "hm. Either you don't know my name and can't let me remember it, or I'm having a senior moment." He sighs. "Ah, dreams, dreams, dreams." He shakes his head. That kindly face, astute and gentle demeanor; he's got a soft warm dark sweater on and with those kindly carpet-gray blue eyes and the sage-paint colored shirt, he looks so gentle like if you found out that he was actually fucking your sister in the bedroom next door, you would swear that someone else got in there even if you were watching you would swear they must have come through some sort of hiccup in the space-time continuum and slipped in when your real kindly grandpa slipped out.

Mr. Dinglepood rocks and smiles, rocks and smiles and says, "You are so trusting. I do hope the AMBLIFOR you took doesn't play with the–vapors—"

"Nah," you say. "Everything is harmless. Harmlesssssss—"

"Ooops," says Mr. Dinglepood. "Slurring your speech again."

"I did?"

Mr. Dinglepood looks a little wary. Then he nods. "Oh, well. But you should remember that you are at the age where deeper awareness—"

You nod. "MaryAnne has told me this. Guess it's true. Guess around this time if there's unresolved stuff, it can come forward in nightmares and dreams."

Mr. Dinglepood nods again. "MaryAnne is smart. At least some of you is aware—a shame to have a bum trip."

"Bum trip?" you ask.

Mr. Dinglepood leans back, folds his hands like a steeple and looks at you over the ridge his steepled hands create. "Tell you some things? Tell you some things that I know are true?"

Industrial Carpet Drag

You nod.

He snaps his fingers and a rocker, like his, appears right next to his. "Siddown and lem'me tell you something." He leans toward you in a kinda cozying-up fashion. "You're a young dude—born, what—32 from 2014 equals—"

"1982—"

"Well," says Mr. Dinglepood, "I heard rumors—" he smiles, "and maybe I saw some stuff." He keeps smiling. "Maybe. Young lady, nineteen or so. At a coffee house, name paid homage to a book by Hubert Selby that came out in the mid-sixties, *The Last Exit to Brooklyn*, only it was actually on Brooklyn Avenue in Seattle, so it was called Last Exit on Brooklyn but that's neither here nor there. The book made quite a stir, kinda compared to stuff by Jack Kerouac. Off the wall, gritty life and sex stuff in New York. Author was never heard from again. Probably couldn't handle sudden fame and fortune. Destroys so many. But again, neither here nor there. Forgive the ramblings of an old man. Back to the story."

You begin to notice something. The pink around you is deepening in color.

"Young lady. She and friends dropped in, sitting, having coffee—poured in the sugar—" Mr. Dinglepood shakes his head. "Never knew what hit her. Sugar laced with LSD. Gone. Just like that. Gone. Mind just—" Mr. Dinglepood snaps his fingers— "gone. Just like that."

You look to Mr. Dinglepood. "Who are you exactly—?"

He just steeples his hands again, looks at you. "So what'd Mr. Blaklavach have to say?"

"Who are you?"

"What did Mr. Blaklavach have to say?"

"Lots of stuff. Liked it when I got mad at him. Like a spider, he had eight eyes but the more angry I got, the less eyes he had. Who are you?"

Mr. Dinglepood just looks at you. "Quite a car ride you had there what with Lana and her Mom. Pretty messed up."

"Yeah, well—who are you?"

"What'd you get out of that?"

The color around you now is an even deeper pink, turning to red.

"So tell me what you got out of that deal with Lana and her mom."

"I'll tell you that when you tell me who you fucking are and what you're saying to me."

"You like MaryAnne," he says.

Not a question, but a statement. "What's it to you?" You back up and say, "Well, yeah—"

"That's good." He snaps his fingers. You feel a presence. And you think you hear someone say, "Hi."

You look around. Just you, the rocking chair, and Mr. Dinglepood in his rocking chair. "And Stan and Peggy. They really like you. You like them?"

"Well—sure—who the hell *are* you?"

"That's good," he says, "that's good. That's very, very good." He snaps his fingers. Again, you feel a presence. Again you look around. No one else there. Just the two of you.

Around you, the color deepens, red to an even a darker red, bordering on purple.

Mr. Dinglepood watches you. "Some people never come here," he says, "some come because they are ready. Some, like you, come out of circumstances not exactly of their choosing but do have some fortunate—" he pauses, choosing his words carefully, "circumstances. Some, like the girl, come here, have no warning—never come back." He sighs, looks away, then after a minute, fixes you with a stare that scares the crap out of you like he's talking directly to your soul and you can't stop him. "So nice to be born to good people but doesn't happen often that good people know how to be good." He laughs. "Human condition, one supposes. But no matter. Coming from a place of no love or trust to a place of love and trust—the Hero's Journey," he says. "The act of supreme nobility when, it seems there is least reason to have faith, we have it anyway. Now that's faith. That is the very definition *of* faith. No matter what, no matter what," and Mr. Dinglepood's voice becomes so soft, so filled with love, so endearing and so infinitely tender, "we come forward to answer life's most courageous call—without wanting to—we come to exist and be these mortal mammals that we are, under this strange sky, under these strange stars. To exist, to be dazzled by being here, to then face our dying. And in the end, we must have faith. We must have faith that we know nothing and that even in our dying we still must have faith that whatever it is to die creates a new birth somewhen, somewhere, else. Unknowable. Unfathomable. Unanswerable. Faith in life's purpose that we are here to do life's bidding and to be the best that we can be and the best of all—is love. No matter what. No matter what the pain. No matter nothing. Faith brings us peace and that it's all right to be here for we are here because of the Universe's call that it is our time to be. And it behooves us to be clear as we can be to discover that purpose and honor it and have gratitude for it. All of this will sustain us throughout lives and through our dying."

Bruce Taylor

You swallow. You feel this prickling sensation in your scalp, your neck. It's like you have stared at the will, the promise of life in the face and you want to cry. From the beauty, from your knowledge of your mortality. You stare at Mr. Dinglepood. You look at that face. You know it. You cannot place it but—you know it.

He stands. It has become dark. "I must go now," he says, "I must go."

You continue to stare at him. "Who are you who are you who *are* you?"

Mr. Dinglepood looks at you. "Life. Life calling forth life. And asking life the most profound question that one can ask. How much do you matter? This time, this place, how much do you matter? What are you willing to do, to matter? To what length will you go to come to rest with knowing that your journey, this place, this time, has brought you your nobility? To what length will you go? Only you can answer that. And answer it you *must*—and answer it—*well.*"

He gives you one long last look. He turns. And all plunges into—blackness.

☠.12.

blackness blackness blackness unbelievable blackness. In the darkness you hear a voice and you recognize it. "My poor Krell . . . could hardly have understood what power was destroying them."

Walter Pidgeon's Morbius of the *Forbidden Planet,* lamenting the loss of the Krell by their unconscious demons, their Monsters From the Id. You suddenly get it; it's never what you know that hurts you. It's what you don't know—refuse to know—that will hurt you—even kill you.

In the blackness you say to yourself: "I am here. Now that I am here, what do I need to know? What am I coming to know? And which way do I go?"

In the darkness, there is nothing. But you slowly turn. A presence. You feel a presence. You do not know what it is but you turn toward—the presence and there, in the distance, a light. You go toward it and you wonder, *Maybe I shouldn't have taken that pill. Maybe that was a bad idea. How am I to know? Maybe all of this, all of this for whatever reason, is exactly what I need to do.*

You move toward the light and before long, you see, seated, a little girl. She must be seven or eight, long red hair, dark eyes, dressed in a simple white cloak, kind of reminding you of a Greek goddess as a little girl. She is seated before a candle and she has her hands palms up, over the candle and above the candle, the Earth slowly, serenely turns.

"Hello," she says. She doesn't look at you. She just sits, watching the Earth turn.

"Who are you?" you ask.

"You. Me. Everyone. But if you really need a name, any name will do. How about Holly?" she says, "Maybe a last name? Something like Gritz? Holly Gritz. I like that. What's in a name? Lana. Stan. Mr. Blaklavach, Mr. Dinglepood. Just sounds, some strange, some not so strange only because they become common sounds. Unusual sounds always scare people. Change is scary." Then she looks at you; a look that is both curious and somehow—ancient. Timeless. She nods. "Sit?"

You sit.

"Yes," says Holly, "sit. Sit a spell and watch the world turn above this candle. Move it too far away—" she does and you can see ice caps advance and sea levels drop. "Move it too close—" she does; the ice vanishes, seas rise, flood the land. "Divine capriciousness," she says. "We all know it. We've always known it. Makes us excited at not knowing anything and makes us frightened at not knowing anything."

"OK," you say, "and which are you?"

She smiles. "Just a little girl with the Earth above her hands. My job this time around."

You really begin to wonder if you should have

taken that sleeping pill, but you don't feel badly—just in a daze. Maybe it's the side effects. Maybe seeing this stuff is a side effect.

She looks at you across an icy North Pole. "What did you learn from Mr. Dinglepood?"

"I learned to ask questions and I guess—to listen."

"What do you want to learn from me?"

"Am I hallucinating?"

Her eyes return to the Earth turning serenely above her hands. "Maybe that's the wrong question to the right answer."

You don't say anything for a long minute but you begin to think you know the meaning of her answer and you say, "There's something I need to know."

"May be no final answer," says Holly.

You watch North America swing into darkness and you can see the lights of cities—there's New York moving into the penumbra, then soon, Chicago, Denver, and finally, Seattle, San Francisco, Los Angeles all seem to go into the darkness at the same time and the lights become more pronounced. "Riddles," you say. You've never liked them because they always make you think you're so damn dumb; everyone else gets them and you don't.

"I know you don't like riddles but you really do know the one that stands the test of time, don't you?"

"Oh, yeah, yeah—" you say, "that one. 'What creature walks on four legs in the morning, two legs at noon and three legs at night?'"

"You know the answer," she says.

Of course you do.

"Of course you do," she says.

She continues to watch the world turn. So much curiosity, so much love, so much admiration in those eyes. "Never get tired," she says. "Been here so long, will be here for a long time. Never, never get tired of this world, how it turns. This little oasis. This 'pale blue dot'. Carl Sagan said that. It took me awhile to arrange things before he could be here but eventually, he came to be and said those words." She looks at you, smiles. "But, my friend, you've '—got promises to keep/And miles to go before you sleep'."

"Robert Frost," you say.

The girl keeps smiling. Finally she says, "You have questions. That's wonderful. So did Oedipus. His questions led him to great pain, but he saw there was an injustice done and to right that injustice, he had to take that journey and even though he discovered himself the cause of the injustice, unconscious as it was, he punished himself for it and so won the favor of the Gods because he was a brave man and sought justice no matter where it led. "

Oh, yeah, you think, oh, yeah. *Yeah, "Oedipus, The King". God, how much the Greeks knew and how much we have forgotten. Wonder if the Krell had some sort of mythology like that?*

"Even if they did," says Holly, "and yes, I can hear your thoughts, but—even if they did, it did not save them from themselves. Were they better for not knowing? Was it better that way? Or is it worse to know what you must come to know—but be powerless to stop it. Then you risk hating yourself for your powerlessness."

"I must come to know something," you say.

"Indeed" says Holly, "as we all must. We all must. But just because we know something doesn't mean we can control it. It just means—we are aware—"

And without thinking you say, "—and we must act

Industrial Carpet Drag

with as much courage as we can for only then can we
be noble, for to know and do nothing—"

The girl looks at you with eyes shining. Then she,
the Earth, the candle fades, fades and—fades away.

☠13.

You are on the sofa and you have got to pee. *Weird dreams*, you think, *I'm glad I know they are dreams.* You get up to go to the bathroom but your pee doesn't go down; it floats up and hangs in mid-air like a little yellow sphere.

Oh, shit, you think. *Oh, dear God.* You walk back out to the living room and the plasma screen TV has sprouted little feet and is taking a shit on the floor; out comes a foul smelling cascade of minute computers, cars, candy. hamburgers, guns, papers, Styrofoam boxes and cups and to top it all off, a violent discharge of CDs, DVDs, and a seeming unending stream of wrapping ribbon in red, white and blue.

"But wait," says the TV, "—there's more!"

And another vile discharge comes from God knows where; stuff that you see sold at midnight that you would only give to your worst enemy. Within minutes, little shoppers appear from somewhere, like roaches, dashing out and carting it all away until there is nothing left.

The TV then sits on the floor, legs crossed. A

Industrial Carpet Drag

message appears on the screen. "Today only, three of anything for the price of one something or thirty percent off from today until today and then twice tomorrow. Buy five! Save three! HurryHurryHurry sale may end but may never end."

You sit there not quite knowing what to think. The TV screen turns a dark blue, then, a voice. "Why are you sitting there and not buying anything?"

This is so, *so* bad but you have to go along with it but how do you go along with something like this? You smile and say, "Freedorg."

Pause. "On sale tomorrow at Jacunuts, in Briquella."

Oh, OK, you think, *so it's on to me.*

"There are laws. We have laws. There are so many laws about not buying anything."

You say nothing. Safest bet. You get up. Your pee has floated out from the bathroom and is following you around, like a round yellow pet. "Go away," you say. "Get in the toilet bowl. Flush yourself away."

The balloon of pee slowly turns a shade of deeper yellow. "You don't want me anymore," it cries plaintively.

"No, no I don't want you anymore. Go 'way!"

"I have always loved you," the pee says. "What did I do to deserve your wanting to get rid of me?"

"I had to get rid of you. I just can't keep accumulating pee in my body—"

"I feel used," says the little spherical pool of pee hovering near your face.

"Because you were the byproduct of food that I ate and so yes, you have been used or something like that." Then you stop. *This is crazy. A TV is sitting in the middle of the floor talking to me and a little pool of my pee doesn't want to leave me alone. Jesus— what was in that fucking sleep medication? I'm more awake than ever.* You look to your watch but the hands have vanished. You go to the balcony and the sky is totally blank. The buildings of the city are upside down. A comet slashes across the heavens and in its wake, the dust and gas spell out, "Sale at Safeway, the next 6.5 nanoseconds only. Five bottles of reality for the price of five! HurryHurryHurry!"

You turn, almost smooshing face first into the little sphere of pee floating nearby.

"Don't you love me anymore?"

God, who's that sound like? Then it occurs to you. *My dad.* You think. *That sounds just like my dad.* Then you stop. *Shit. That sounds like me when Julia left. I was what—twenty five? She accused me of hovering, smothering, of not letting her have space—*

"—are you angry at me?" says the little ball of pee.

You don't say anything. You don't want to say anything. This is getting really fucking uncomfortable—

Bink! The TV comes on. Your dad on TV and he's looking—right at you. "Only you understand me," he says. "Don't leave me. Don't leave me like your mother left me. We're buddies, aren't we?"

You recoil. Then—Oh, oh—you sit on the sofa. Oh- oh—you look back at the TV and a giant mosquito looks out at you—"Eeeeee. Heeeellllllpp meeeeeeeee." The mosquito has turned into a fly stuck in a web and the face is that of your father and a spider with the face of your mother is coming down toward him—

You close your eyes. When you open them there is a stately fellow, white haired, dressed in a white robe, looking at you. He's standing behind the TV, leaning forward, his weight resting on folded arms on top of the television. "Yes, it's hard," he says, "and it gets harder still—but now that I've discovered that I've married my mother and killed my father—" His hands move toward his eyes.

The little ball of your pee floats nearby screaming beseechingly—"Don't you love me anymore—save me! Help me! Help meeeeee!"

You clap your hands over your eyes, then your ears and in a second, it's quiet. You cautiously open your eyes, take your hands from your ears—"Heeeelp meeeee—don't leeeaaaave meeeeeee!"

You again clap your hands over your ears, clamp your eyes shut and this time you just fucking wait. And you wait. And finally again, you cautiously open your eyes, pull your hands away from your ears. Quiet. The TV is off, no sphere of pee is floating around. *It's over,* you think. *Jesus Christ, how dreadful. I just want to sleep.* It does occur to you that if this is a dream, then you are indeed asleep. But since you're walking around, you must now be awake. Sighing, you go out to the balcony to look at the nighttime view.

Seattle is still upside down.

☠14.

You sit back down. OK. You're in some sort of dream, so if you lay down again, you'll be asleep, which is what you are already experiencing. Somehow, you realize, this makes no real sense, but if you're in a dream, then if you'll fall asleep in a dream, maybe it will really take you to really being really asleep. Or something like that. You look at your watch. Still no hands. Gotta be about three but you are just not sure. You wonder, *Should I turn on the TV and see what Dream TV is dishing up?* No, you decide against it. *Let me be awake to see what it is. It will just be screwed up again if I sleep.* You also know this isn't quite like a dream and it'd be scary because it feels like you have no control, as if something else is going on that creates this place you keep going to—and you wonder and you wonder: *Is MaryAnne right? That there comes a time that, whether you want it or not, you get insight? Is that what this is? Is that all that this is?* You remember Mr. Dinglepood talking about that girl who got hit with the acid without knowing it. Is it the not knowing that used to be called "bad trips"?

94

Industrial Carpet Drag

—you see yourself grabbing Dr. Morbius and yelling at him, "That's your monster, Morbius and your Krell beast will use whatever it takes to melt through that steel to get to you—"

—*it's Oedipus all over again, isn't it?*—you ponder—forced by our desire to know, forced by circumstances to come to know the nature of The Shadow and forced to take responsibility—what about that girl who got the acid in the sugar?

—she wasn't looking. She wasn't expecting anything. She had no idea. Was that the difference? Had she been on a quest, had she been seeking—would the impact have been the same? Bum trip instead of a bad trip? Detour instead of going off the cliff? Whacked by a lion instead of devoured by it? What would have happened to Morbius had he never acknowledged the Krell beast as his own Id? What would have happened to Morbius had he refused to see?

—you're back to the place of darkness and in the distance a bright light and as you move forward, you see a candle, you see the Earth suspended above it but the little girl isn't there. You approach and your eyesight suddenly becomes so powerful that you can see the planet's surface and every square inch—peoplepeoplepeople—ten billion, twelve billion fourteen billion—the planet begins to glow—

"—solid Krell Metal, inches thick . . . that machine is going to supply your monster with whatever amount of power it requires to reach us," says Commander Adams.

—the doors melt, flake away, the dials on the displays in the control room in the Krell science lab go crazy, as they show the entire energy of the planet being used to create Morbius's unconscious Krell beast coming after its creator, Dr. Morbius—

—you watch the Earth glow red, you hear the screams of 14 billion 15 billion 16 billion people, the animals, the oceans boil and—

—Earth melts, the atmosphere evaporates, the oceans flash to steam—in a bright and sparkling flash—

—if Morbius doesn't want to know—if Oedipus doesn't want to know—if we don't want to know, to dare to take responsibility—*flash*—

—*flashFLASHFLASHFLASH—KA-POW KAPOW RUMBLERUMBLE*

—you jerk awake and go "OH—SHITOH SHITOHSHIT!" then part of you says, "We've been through this before." You curl up on the sofa and the TV is on and you struggle to remember, *Did I turn it on? Did I turn it off?* You can't remember.

"—Chicago continues to clean up," says the announcer, "—three more tornadoes overnight and even the Willis Tower has extensive damage. Commuter train torn off its track and seventy dead as it was thrown into an oncoming train—Detroit with eighteen inches of hail and in Seattle, at this hour, looks like totally unexpected severe weather to hit—residents there are urged—"

—in rapid succession on the TV, loud staccato *blipbliblipblip* designed to get your attention and the bottom scrawl, bright red, reads SEVERE WEATHER ALERT SEVERE WEATHER ALERT SEATTLE BELLEVUE TACOMA AND WESTERN WASHINGTON UNEXPECTED SEVERE WEATHER OUTBREAK TORNADO WARNINGS IN EFFECT DAMAGING WINDS HAIL SEEK SHELTER

Industrial Carpet Drag

"—Morbius, that thing out there. It's *you!*"

FLASHCRASH KA-POW KA-POW rumble RUMBLERUMBLEROAR CRASHpat-taptaprattle RATTLECRACKLE-RATTLE-BANGBANGBANG—

—you just can't get upset—a dream before, a dream now—*what the fuck musta been in that over-the-counter—*

FLASHFLASHFLASH KA-POW KA-BLOOWIE

—*boy, fucking vivid dream*—you open your eyes—*yeah, and the screen will be blank 'cause I know I turned that—*

blipblipblip that staccato blipping from the TV. SEVERE WEATHER ALERT SEVERE LIGHTNING HAIL DAMAGING WINDS REPORTED IN PORTLAND, OLYMPIA SEVERE WEATHER INTENSIFYING TORNADO ALERT SEEK SHELTER *blipblipblip, blipblipblip, blipblipblip*

—*oh, for fucking crying out loud! This is fucking Seattle, this is just a fucking dream like I had before. Just not possible shouldn't have taken that shit maybe it is in some weird way combining with the carpet fumes—but what a hoot—get an automatic high just by walking into a new building.*

—*KA-RASH!*—The whole place shakes and you sit bolt upright and look out the sliding glass door and the sky is alive with fire and something in Seattle is engulfed in flames that boil up to the flashing sky—

—*a dream? Hallucination again? Reality—?*

WHOOOROOOOOAAAAAARRRRRRRRRRUM MMBLERUMBLERUMBLE.

Your hair stands on end. Seattle is not upside down, there is no pool of pee floating nearby, the TV is where it's supposed to be—that sound, that fucking weird sound like a freight train—you suddenly leap up, bolt downstairs and go to the safest place you can think of—you grab piles of blankets and wrestle past boxes to dive beneath the kitchen table in the corner and pile the blankets over you and the place shakes and even where you are you can hear what has to be hail pounding everything around you and you whimper, "Ohshitohshitohshit—"

Suddenly, quiet. You realize you are shaking so violently that it becomes an uncontrollable seizure and you shake and spasm uncontrollably, aware but unable to stop the seizing and finally, finally, finally that subsides.

Finally, you're able to crawl out from your makeshift hidey-hole, sore-muscled and aching and scared out of your wits and stumble to the front door—a fallen tree blocks your way. Miraculously, the floodlights remain on. A foot of hail, the size of golf-balls—everywhere. A poplar tree across the middle of the Subie has the car's front lifted up like a dark sausage squeezed in the middle; its windows busted out from the hail and a house, not far away—well, the house that was supposed to be there—gone. Nobody comes out of other houses—probably still too frightened, you think. Then slowly, the door opens to the townhome just down the multiple driveway and an older guy cautiously looks out—

—in the light you see he's wearing pajamas with Mickey Mouse in various poses all over it and—

—Mickey says, "H-h-hi folks—" in that typical high pitched mouse voice and from somewhere, all the characters of Walt Disney's imagination come flooding out from behind the guy and they begin dancing in the street and in the distance, the darkness fades into an image of a spaceport and a huge rocket sitting there, the design and concept based on the well-known advice of Werner von Braun, whose rocketry got its start with the Nazis who had him work, developing V-2 technology to bomb Great Britain, well, we don't talk about that do we? His glorified multi-stage V-2 now stands on the launch pad and you hear a voice from somewhere, "—from Walt Disney, this is *Walt Disney Presents* and tonight, from 'Tomorrowland,' be with us as we explore the frontiers of science, where, in the near future, we may well have colonies on the moon and the first manned exploration of Mars—"

—wasn't too long ago you saw a retrospective of that series that had such an impact on American Culture—Walt Disney—one man can Make a Difference. Werner von Braun—yes, indeed. One man almost made a huge difference had the Germans developed the atomic bomb and fit it on the V-2 rocket but that's all behind us and you see scenes of those wonderful ships, somewhere in the not too distant future, certainly no later than 1975, heading off to Mars, to finally orbit Mars; then with the scene of explorers on the planet discovering relics of an ancient civilization with architectural skeletons built by vanished Martians marching off into the distance—

—you sit up on the sofa, rub your face and say, "—knew it was a fucking dream. Just knew it." You look to your watch. Three a.m. *The sleeping stuff must be wearing off,* you think. TV is off. Main light in the kitchen area still on. You stumble to the balcony. Pleasant evening, moon beyond noon position, heading toward moonset in the next few hours. Seattle looks just swell. You breathe in. Air feels good. You open the slider more.

Maybe now, you think, *maybe now I can just fucking sleep.* You start sneezing again. Look to your hand, a little bit of blood, nothing much. *Getting better* you think, *getting better. Maybe the worst is over.*

You find yourself really thirsty. The only thing in the place—water and—beer. You go to the Wein-Glaz fridge, grab a beer and start chugging and about two-thirds of the way through—you stop. You stumble to the bathroom, look at the over-the-counter medication of the AMBLIFOR and read, "Alcohol may enhance effects of AMBLIFOR—use in moderation."

You shrug. No problem. You finish the beer, you turn on the plasma TV, wondering about the latest from Chicago. The announcer is a young lady with a tight blue top and she's got blonde hair, and her look is serious. "—and more tornadoes apparently touched town in Chicago just a few minutes ago. Hail up to eighteen inches deep has buried parts of Detroit and ten inches of rain in thirty minutes have led to high water, flash flooding in Cincinnati. Severe winds with gusts up to l10 mph have blown trucks off the road on Interstate 90 outside Butte, Montana, while around Portland, Oregon, there were 500 lightning strikes in the last hour—here's Marty Stanford from the CNN Weather Center—"

There is a split image on the screen, the anchorwoman on the left, Marty Stanford on the right, with an image of the US on a screen behind him.

"So, what is going on?" asks the anchorwoman. "Looks like a lot of severe weather."

Marty laughs. "Oh, we've got some active weather right now; jet stream is taking an unusual pattern bringing us all sorts of interesting weather and pesky storms though it is a bit unusual to see Chicago hit by severe tornadoes since there has never been such an outbreak like this before but it's not entirely out of the question—"

"But we've been seeing a lot of this recently," persists the anchorwoman, probably going off script. You know she's gonna be reprimanded for that. Certainly Marty is caught off-guard by her directness and looks unprepared—

"Well, it is late spring and we can see this type of activity but it isn't entirely without precedent—"

Oh-oh—you think, *this anchorwoman is gonna get canned real fast.*

"But doesn't it seem like there has been so much more of this, world-wide?" she asks. "We just lost another jumbo-jet as it was flying from New Zealand and hit turbulent weather near the southern coast of Malaysia just minutes away from landing at Kuala Lumpur—"

"Well," says Marty who looks like he really wishes someone would leap on the news desk at CNN headquarters and drag that fucking anchorwoman off the set and replace her with a programmed robot, "that appears to have been related to the sensor that mis-read the vapor content of the atmosphere and the computers failed to compensate for jet speed—"

You know the message here. Make it human error. Gotta be human error. Don't make it about horrendous weather making flying a form of Russian Roulette or suicide. Flying is a multi-billion dollar industry and we got planes to build, routes to fly, and if the atmosphere gets fucked up, that's just the price of doing business but *don't* confuse the flying public with the reality that flying is fucking over. You study

Bruce Taylor

Marty Stanford and you fancy you can see a desperation in his eyes—you wonder if he's unconsciously saying to himself, "I'm just a fucking TV weatherman—don't confront me I'm not here to deliver anything substantial—I'm here to entertain. Someone for the love of fucking GOD take this cunt anchorbitch out of my face someone shut her up! We're not here to give news we're not here to make people think. If people really thought, they wouldn't buy any of the shit the sponsors have us try to sell as if it's shit you just canNOT do without and you just have to have or your lives are meaningless. Take this cunt off the air and don't let her back on I can't answer her questions 'cause I don't know and I don't care to know cause I'm too fucking *scared* to know—"

"—OK," says the anchorwoman, realizing that she has just probably lost her job and is going to have to fuck a lot of managers and give a few blow jobs to get it back. Hand jobs just ain't gonna do it this time around but that's the price you pay for being really gutsy and trying to say something of merit. "Thanks to our weather man Marty Stanford, keeping us on top of the current weather and after this announcement, we'll return with the latest news on the breakup of the marriage of new rising star, OhMee Bohner and his ex-wife to be, Seemy Puzzzie. And after that, it's alcohol rehab for Emmy Award winning singer, Eeton Beehvherr— "

It's a commercial about getting rid of all those hairy areas on your body by use of Maj-Ick Remover, a device that Painlessly! Effortlessly! No Muss! No Fuss! Takes hair away by Patented Technology! So you can look as hairless as a child and be sexually desirable.

Industrial Carpet Drag

In a few minutes, the news returns. The anchorwoman who was there before the break, is gone. *Probably lost her job*, you think, *for being real. Maybe she was taken out and shot. Maybe she stepped outside for a smoke or a joint and was clobbered by a five inch hail-stone. Maybe when she went to use the can, as she was sitting, the sewers suddenly and catastrophically backed up and she was impaled on the ceiling of the john by a geyser of shit. Who knows. Who the fuck*—you begin to feel a little woozy—not bad, but it's kinda like you're floating—can't think clearly—*where the fuck*—*maybe I shouldn't have had*—

—you don't know where you are. But you feel a presence, that presence. You're glad it's there 'cause man, you don't know where you are. It isn't light, it isn't dark and you look down. Like you're standing on a surface and you touch it. Not warm, not cold. Everything is neutral. You take a breath. That—presence. You feel it more over to your right and that's the direction you begin walking. And before long—it's Mr. Blaklavach. He's still got two eyes. He smiles faintly.

"Mr. Blaklavach—" you say.

He shakes his head—just points.

You nod. You continue on. Before long, you come to Mr. Dinglepood. He looks at you. And you swear to God, you know him. And you look at him. "I know you. I know who you are."

Mr. Dinglepood just shakes his head. You understand. Not now. Not yet. He points.

You continue on. *I know him*, you think, *I know him. Who is he? It's not Mr. Dinglepood—it's—it's—damn*—

But before you can ponder farther, you see that little girl. She splits off, becoming two little girls. The one on the right looks at you and then removes her hands from beneath the Earth. She stands, then leaves. You watch the polar caps shrinking, you hear the shriek of billions of people as they are creating more billions and within that scream, the shriek of all life and the flash-hiss of oceans flashing to steam and the Earth melts.

The other little girl sits there, with a look somewhere between imploring and grief and yet still hopeful, her hands above the flame of the candle, protecting, protecting. But you wonder, how much longer can she offer protection if we don't—can't—won't—

It hits you like a brick: *You can't know what you don't know.* You gulp. *How do you come to know what you don't know? How do you even know that you must come to know what you don't know?*

Suddenly, you are aware of someone approaching and you hear, "You look around."

You turn. A tall fellow stands there, tall and gangly, with long hair; he smiles. "'Twas brillig," he says, "and the slithy toves

Did gyre and gimble in the wabe;

All mimsy were the borogoves,

And the mome raths outgrabe."

He tilts his head. You walk with him. You point back with your thumb. "Alice?" you ask.

He shrugs. "Alice in the Wonderland of life. Alice discovering the nature of Choice? I don't know." He smiles. It's a Cheshire grin. You know who this is and you've read everything about him, as well as Kafka, Dickens, Sophocles and T.S. Eliot when you were at the University, debating whether or not writing was an option for you.

And you dare ask the loaded question. You stop and you look at Lewis Carroll and you dare ask the question. "What is it you had to come to know—"

He turns. He does not want to answer that question. "I don't know," he says.

"You know what history says about you."

"I know," he says. "They're wrong."

"You know the suspicions history has about you."

He turns, enraged. "What of it? What of it? Does it make my work any less?"

You stop, stunned. "You don't care? How can you write something so loving and caring and—not care?"

Carroll turns, contemptuous. "Be gone! Be gone! This is none of your affair. I did nothing improper." He turns, strides away, stops and turns again. "How dare you even insinuate that I—" his words become lost in rage, his face contorted, his eyes narrow.

"Dude," you say, "isn't it your responsibility to address how you are seen by others? Your impact? That it tarnishes your art?"

His look softens, then abruptly changes and he begins laughing. "It mattered little when I lived; it matters not at all that I am gone. People read my work and love what I've done. Let people believe what they want."

"That your interest in children, particularly Alice, may not have been the most literarily motivated? You want that legacy?"

Carroll still smiles. "Even if your crude accusations were of some merit," he says, "you think I can do anything about them? This conversation has no basis in reality save it is just your imaginings. I'm gone, dead lo these many years. And remember, remember, think of me as you like but also know that I cannot defend myself. And shame on you. Happily, children, and all the Alices that have been and are yet to be, will take great joy in my play."

He walks off, disappears, and you are left with you don't-know-what. Except that dead people really can't defend themselves but it is, nonetheless, worthy of investigation into how much people really don't or can't or won't investigate their own motives and how unconscious people really can be. The question is, you ponder, if faced with the choice of wanting to know or not wanting to know things about oneself that may be difficult—how many people would really take the challenge? And yet, by not wanting to look—the voice of Walter Pidgeon, aka Morbius, comes back to you, "My poor Krell . . . they could hardly have understood what power was destroying them."

Is that better, you think, *considering the little girl getting up to leave the Earth to self-destruct—than knowing and watching one self-destruct anyway?* You suspect that, of the two, the latter is far, far more painful than the former. How indeed do you have serenity over those things that you cannot or are not—able to change? How do you witness self-destruction and be at peace with that?

You ponder this as you continue walking and presently, you come upon another figure, slumped over in the form of abject depression and despair. Beside him, a finished manuscript—*Madame Bovary*. You sit beside the figure, "Gustave?" You say, "Gustave Flaubert?"

He does not respond. You pick up the manuscript and start reading it. It's an excellent translation, every word, syllable—perfect, "It is said," you continue, as you admire the perfection of the work, "that you spent the morning putting the comma in and the afternoon taking it out."

"Oui." So soft a voice, "Oui, that is probably not far from the truth."

"You must be very proud."

Gustave does not look up. "Oui—yes, of that yes—"

"But—?"

"It's a feat that has great and grave consequences."

You shake your head. "Who would not die an easy death knowing that they had created such beauty, such a testament to art that would give them the title of the author that had written the most perfect book?"

"Indeed. I will never know if this was right or not for while I am—" he sighs, "satisfied, one would guess for being so known—I also did something I so regret—"

Oh, yeah, you think, *yeah, so it is true.*

With voice heavy and aching, aching with remorse and regret—"I turned my back on love." He laughs. "I wrote of love but turned my back on love."

"Oh, yeah," you whisper, "so it's true—while you were writing the great work, there was a woman you loved but you were too busy to have time for her, to return her love—and unexpectedly—she died."

"That is true, my friend. That is true. The last years of my life were misery and even now, even here, the misery, unabated. I did not know. How could I not know? What was I thinking of? I thought I was doing the right thing but the cost, the cost, the cost."

You stand. *Such love*, you think, *such love.* You walk a few paces, *such love—to have someone love—*

It hits you like a sledgehammer to your skull. You fall forward; the ground turns to clear glass and you are looking down, to see yourself at nineteen with your soul mate, Michalene. It's a summer's day in June, thirteen years earlier, 2001 and you are looking down on yourself as Michalene looks to you and says, crying, "You don't know how to love. I want you and you don't know how to love."

As you look down on yourself, you find yourself suddenly weeping, then pounding the glass, "Bryce! Bryce! Bryce!" you yell, "Say something, stupid! She's beautiful. She's all you could ever hope for! Say something! Anything! But don't let her go, you idiot! She loves you with heart, soul and body and you know you love her why the hell can't you tell her that! Don't let her go! You'll regret it for the rest of your life!"

But, dismally, you watch yourself say nothing except, "I'm sorry, I guess you're right—" And guiltily, you watch her turn, walk away in the setting sun and you say to that image of yourself, through the years, "All you would have had to have done was to say, 'I love you, I care about you and I'm willing to fight for this love—' And you did not."

You watch from above, you see your tears splash on the glass as you watch her walking away from you—because *you* turned your back—on love.

☠.15.

You sit there on that glass a long, long time. The tears have long since dried. "Why?" you ask, "How could I have done that?"

You come back to the here and now, with that question in your head. It is a question you've asked yourself so many times. You have wondered about her so often. You have imagined her making love with someone else and it has always made you so, so sad.

You drift in that VOC/paint-fume/ alcohol/AMBLIFOR/The Right Time of Life hormone haze and you wonder. *Why now?* You suspect it has an awful lot to do with your family of origin stuff— that Michalene was too different, too "unfamiliar"—not family. Then, you ponder, *What it is about my family—if I don't get this, I might lose MaryAnne too—like so many that I have lost.*

Something. Something. Something about all this, the crummy apartment, the not-so-hot-job, something. You lie there wondering. *This is what I must come to know. How do I come to know that which I don't know I must come to know?*

You feel a presence. A voice. Sounds like Peggy, no—MaryAnne—"—easy, you can only know so much—easy, easy—"

BreepBreep goes the phone on the coffee table. You recognize the number. MaryAnne.

"Hi," you say, "I was just thinking—"

"Oh my God," she whispers, "are you OK? I've been trying to get you for the last thirty minutes—"

You glance to your watch. Fifteen minutes? It's two a.m.—you've totally lost track of time, thinking it was much later. "Yeah," you say, "I'm OK—"

"—I thought you'd call—I've been so worried—"

"—huh?" you say. "What—?"

Long pause. "You couldn't have slept—" The incredulity in her voice startles you.

"—what—?"

"The storm, the tornado—"

Oh, God, you think, *the dream is repeating. This is just like the last one I had.* You try this instead. "I've been having these weird dreams of storms and tornadoes hitting Seattle—"

"BRYCE!" yells MaryAnne, "THIS ISN'T A DREAM—"

??Didn't someone say that in the last dream?

"—turn on the television—it's all over the news— I'd come over there but the streetlights are out and the roads are impassable. Hey, if you don't believe, look outside."

You've heard that in the last couple of dreams, too. All it's about is your anxiety about global warming crap playing with your head. That's all, but nonetheless, you flip on the TV and on the bottom of the image, a bright red crawl says, "BREAKING NEWS EXTREME WEATHER PORTLAND AND

Industrial Carpet Drag

SEATTLE HIT BY APPARENT TORNADOES. EIGHT INCHES OF HAIL FALL IN BELLINGHAM. HOOD CANAL BRIDGE CLOSED PENDING INSPECTION AFTER 110 MPH GUSTS HIT SPAN. DO NOT GO OUTSIDE DO NOT DRIVE then the crawl begins to repeat.

"Bryce? You OK? You there?"

"—uh—yeah but this was just like the other two dreams—"

"BRYCE! GO OUTSIDE AND *LOOK*!"

"OK. Back in a minute."

"I'll stay on the line."

You don't know what to think. You were out there earlier and it looked real and it wasn't. Last time you opened the door—you open the door. A tree blocks your way. Outside, hail up to five inches deep, hail as big as golf balls. The Subie SVX scrunched in the middle by a fallen tree and over there, three or four houses away—where a house once was—just the foundation.

You turn and slam the door. The confusion is overwhelming. You look inside the garage and there, in the corner, a table overturned and blankets. *Ohmigod! Ohmigod! It really DID happen!* You stumble back upstairs, grab the phone. "OK. OK, OK," your hand trembles as you speak, "OK, it really did happen. I really did run downstairs and cover myself up, and when I went outside—I saw a guy and—I don't remember much after that except I woke up on the sofa—" You are now totally confused. "I took an Amblifor to try to sleep—then later, had some beer—"

You hear this exasperated sigh. "Amblifor isn't as harmless as they say. People have hallucinated on it and having alcohol—" She sighs again. "So you're OK."

"Yeah," you say. "What about you?"

"Thought the skylights were going to go. Oh, so scary and the noise! And the winds—guess we had some gusts around here close to 85. Probably find a lot of shingles blown off and I know one of the trees down the block went down." A short pause. "Silver lining. It was blocking my view of Mt. Rainier." She laughs. "Not anymore. I'll have my view back." She laughs again.

"Sure you're OK," you ask.

"Yeah. Yeah. Not going to get much sleep, though."

"Me neither," you say, "but gonna try. Exhausted by all this moving and these dreams have just been so weird."

"Ever hear the name of a story called, 'In Dreams Begin Responsibilities?' It's by Delmore Schwartz. If you haven't read it, read it some time."

"Huh," you say, "studied English, but haven't run across that."

"Anyway," says MaryAnne, "let's talk tomorrow."

"Yeah. I'll be in a better place—I think. I hope. G'night."

"'night."

☠16.

You can't believe it. You just ca-NOT believe it. You go to the balcony. It's cold and hailstones the size of golf balls sit there. Yes, the storm *did* happen and when you saw the guy in the—he couldn't have been wearing Mickey Mouse pj's—could he? Something about him—you tripped again. As if sleepwalking, you go downstairs, open the door. Flood lights are on, tree still blocking the exit, Subie SVX still scrunched up in the back, windows busted out and the U-Haul truck's windows also busted out. *Ohhhhhhh shit*. And you can guess what is going to happen next and you fucking DREAD what is going to happen next. You go back upstairs. *Oh, well*, you think. *Maybe dreams can anticipate— maybe somehow this is to prepare—can dreams do that? Maybe they can, Sure hope so.*

BrrepBreepBrrep cell phone rattling away on the coffee table and you have this just dreadful premonition as to what this is going to be about. And you hope it isn't, but if it is—*why oh why couldn't it have been a dream*, you wonder. *Oh, crap.*

"Bryce," *Ah, shit! Yeah, it's Stan. Here we go.*

"Stan—I know—"

"—just got up here and got the early news—holycatz—a tornado?"

"One or two depending on where you were at. One hit Portland I think, another one here. Close to here. Really, really close to here—"

Pause. "*How* close?"

"*Real* close."

"Damage?"

You're prepared. "To the house, from the inside, everything looks fine but probably shingles missing. Apparently it touched down just a block or so from here. Subie got scrunched."

OK, Yup. Here it comes.

"WHAT? WHAT? WHY DIDN'T YOU FUCKING PUT IT IN THE GARAGE WHY'D YOU LEAVE IT OUTSIDE—"

He goes on like that for a while and when he is trying to get air to bluster and sputter some more, you say—and you suddenly think, *ah-ha—I have learned something*—you say, "Stan, cool down. No one had any idea when the storm was going to hit. Nobody. And two, there was so much stuff in the garage that I couldn't have parked it!" *Here it comes, volley two*, you think.

"WHEN YA SAW THE STORM COMING, YOU COULDA MOVED STUFF OUT OF THE WAY YOU COULDA MOVED THE CAR IN—" And he goes on and on and how he goes on and you just wait until he has to catch his breath again and you say, "Stan? Hey, Stan? There was no time, there was way too much stuff, I was asleep when it hit, I had no idea and nobody had any idea. It came out of the blue—" You sigh and pause. "I know you're upset. I would be too. I am sorry."

Industrial Carpet Drag

He doesn't say anything. Just breathes.

You say, "Are you all right? I saw you got more crap happening there—"

"Yeah, shit, it's a mess—we have to be here at least three more days. More possibility of this shit happening tomorrow. Oh, hey, here's Peggy—"

"Hi," she says, "You OK?"

"What can I say?" you say. "It was just—wow."

"We heard about it just a few minutes ago. Tried calling but got a busy signal."

"Yeah, talking to MaryAnne—she wanted to come over but lights are out, streets closed, crap all over the roads, still got inches of hail everywhere."

"I heard Stan yelling—um—guess the Subie got it, huh?"

You want to cry. *That* hasn't changed. "Oh, God, Peggy," you say. "I am so sorry—if I'd known—but no one knew. The forecast was for great weather, the garage was packed—"

"Hey," she says, oh, the sweet milky voice that melts your heart, "it happens, What's to say? We all have to stick together now. If we are learning anything from all of this, it's that our lavish attention to individualism and materialism has to get tossed. We have to go tribal if we are going to survive. I'm afraid we are in for one long, rough ride."

"Yeah," you say. "Be that as it may, I'm still really sorry about your car." You still want to cry. "But the place, at least from the inside is OK. When it gets light, I'll look at it from the outside. What'd your news have to say about it?"

"Said the damage was severe, estimated both tornadoes to be at least F l, but probably more like a two."

You laugh. "Wow. I thought the geography prevented anything like that from happening here but—guess not. Not anymore."

"Yeah," she says, "like all bets are off now. Well, now that we're up, guess we're going to stay up. Cleaning up more stuff up around the outside. God, tree limbs, over- turned cars, some of the roof peeled away. Even the Sears Tower got it and a lot of the high rises have windows blown out. Crap all over the streets." She says something to Stan, covers the phone then returns. "We'll touch base later. Look around and tell us what you find."

"OK," you say. "It's three a.m. here, going to try to get more sleep, barring more tornadoes."

Short laugh. "Hope not. Take care and don't worry, OK?"

"OK. Bye. Thanks"

You hold on to the cell phone, look out the sliders to Seattle. The clouds have cleared away, the moon is lower, brighter, so lovely, so serene, and you cry. Again. Anyway.

☠.17.

After a while, you think, *I just have to get more sleep* but you decide to check out the local 24 cable station and see what they say about what happened. The crawl at the bottom moves on, kind of reminding you of *The Rubiayat of Omar Khayyam* but you fix it up a bit: "The moving crawl writes and having writ/Comes not back to cancel half a line or cancel any word of it."

BREAKING NEWS: SEVERE WEATHER UPDATE; TWO CONFIRMED TORNADOES HAVE TOUCHED DOWN IN WESTERN WASHINGTON, ONE SOUTH OF SEATTLE, ONE IN NORTH SEATTLE AND ONE IN PORTLAND DAMAGE LOCALIZED BUT EXTENSIVE. HIGH WINDS DAMAGE I-90 FLOATING BRIDGE HAIL DAMAGES MANY BUILDINGS. PEOPLE ADVISED TO STAY HOME STAY TUNED FOR FURTHER UPDATES STORMS TOTALLY UNFORESEEN FORECASTERS AT A LOSS AT SUDDEN APPEARANCE.

And while this crawl goes on, the weather gal, Molly Floofy, is blabbering away like she's talking

117

about the ingredients for Jell-O: "—well, everyone was certainly surprised by this wild and wacky weather—" She looks like she's about nineteen, lives in a sorority; bland, blonde haired and brainless as a turnip. "Gosh," she says, "it was quite a night, hail, lightning and looks like a couple of funnel clouds dropped down to do a little damage."

You think, *A little damage, you fucking eye-candy weather bimbo. That was Peggy's beloved Subie and a 540K house that got ripped off its foundation— probably sitting in pieces all over Wallingford. A little damage. Why the hell don't you come out and look for yourself or will the wind damage your makeup and eye shadow—*

"—you'd never guess anything like this was going to come our way but it looks like something came roaring through the Columbia Gorge and just exploded all over Western Washington—there had been turbulent weather on the east side of the Cascades but there was no indication it was going to move, much less move as rapidly to the west as it did—but—" and she smiles brightly, as if she's talking about Barbie Dolls, "—that's what you get when you live in the good ol' Northwest—" and she giggles and you turn off the TV.

You go to the kitchen and not finding any glasses, grab a plastic sports bottle. You glance at the bottom and see the little American Plastics pyramid stamped in the bottom and inside it: "7" *Huh.* you think, *wasn't there something about plastics leaching something out in the liquids stored in bottles with the number "7" on the bottom? Thought I heard something—I'm surprised Peggy—*you look at the bottle. *Oh. It's mine. Oh, well. One of these days.* You see there's still water

Industrial Carpet Drag

in there and you think it's been there for a few days but it should be fine and you gulp it down and fill the bottle and drink from it again. You've had the bottle forever, used it for hiking—boy, it's been everywhere. You realize as you think about it, it's funny how something like an innocent water bottle can anchor you to the here and now. You also notice that you're feeling a little more clear-headed. And then you notice that it's actually kind of cool in here. And then you notice something else. It's a little drafty.

Oh-oh. You really want to sleep some more but— you look around. The slider to the deck is closed. Nothing open on the second floor. Downstairs, first floor OK, pretty well protected. That means—

Up on the third floor, yeah, colder. Guest room OK. Stan and Peggy's bedroom, that's OK, bathroom—oh, man—lower part of the bathroom window punched out by—there, on the floor, huge hailstones—must have been three inches across. You look up. Skylight cracked. *Oh, man*, you think, *oh, man. Nothing I can do about this right now*. You close the door. *Maybe if that's all the damage we got, we're lucky,* you think. *Bet some shingles are gone.*

Down to the living room, on the sofa—you do feel calmer and maybe the inadvertent airing out of the place has a silver lining. You aren't sneezing.

So you lie down again. Warm up fast. You sleep and—

—you and Stan are hiking last summer up Aasgard Pass to the Enchantment Plateau, the place where Peggy ate her Harvest Granola bar while you collapsed and Stan threw up. She's got that really cool hydration system built into her new Rockies JanSport Pack, the Platypus plastic bottle fits in the back pocket

119

and has a tube that comes out of the top, over the pack and clips neatly on the shoulder strap, so all you have to do is flip up the end piece, bite down on it and that squeezes open the pressure valve which kind of looks like the slit in the head of a dick where the pee comes out. You like that idea. "That's really slick," you say to Peggy. "Reaching around for my water bottle is a real pain. Been thinking about that."

You sit there with Peggy, staring at the stark grandeur of the Upper Enchantments, to the gray rubble of glacier-busted angular rock, the muddy melt pools, the steep snowfields embracing and clutching the high cliffs of Snow Creek Wall and Snow Creek Glacier. You're glad to be recovering. Stan, it looks like it's gonna take him a bit of time. He sits, knees up, hands clasping his knees and looking like he's been sucker punched. Occasionally, he drinks Gatorade to get his electrolytes electrolyting a little better.

Peggy sips out of her hydration system. "Yeah," she says, and she grins, digging it, the view, being here, the blue sky, the rocks, the glaciers and everything else under that sudden and soundless blue of sky. And then she says, "Yeah. I don't miss those plastic bottles at all. Especially after all that news that came out about them some years back."

"Huh?" you say.

"Saw it years ago in the *Seattle Times*. A chemical, I think it's BPA—used in plastics, leached out into water. Turned out to be a hormone disrupter? I'm not sure but it looked like it mimicked hormones so you had frogs with three legs, fish that were both male and female—really weird crap happened and it was finally and absolutely traced to that stuff." She points to your bottle.

Industrial Carpet Drag

"Great," you say, "poisoned again."

Peggy peels back the wrapper of her Harvest Bar and breaks off a piece. "Want some?"

"Sure, thanks."

"Amazing how toxic the environment has gotten. Back in 2012, it was said there were eighty-thousand man-made chemicals in the environment and only two-hundred of which were tested for human safety." She laughs, shakes her head. "God knows how much worse it is now. No wonder people are having more chronic health problems."

You look to your green plastic bottle. You wonder. *Am I developing ovaries? Are my breasts enlarging?*

She takes another bite of the energy bar as she sits on that rectangular busted chunk of granite which looks ethereal as hell and if Peggy's in heaven, which she looks like she is—which you know you are—though Stan looks like he's just suddenly come up from the lowest rung in Dante's *Inferno* and is suffering the existential bends. You look at Peggy. The love of life burns through her, and you know that no matter where she is, she's in heaven. Now, now from this standpoint you can understand why the dream of Michalene was so painful. She was very much like Peggy—

—in the present, you squirm on the couch but then you go back to the reverie of being in the Enchantments and Peggy, luminous, loving everything.

You, sitting there with her, get re-energized enough to truly appreciate the raw beauty but also wondering about your water bottle and resolving to get a new one from REI ASAP which you didn't do. Now, you're wondering. Back then, upon the

Enchantment Plateau, you were beginning to wonder. "Really," you say to Peggy, pointing to your water bottle, "that serious?"

"Guess so," she says. She turns, rummages in her pack, and produces licorice. Her eating makes you realize that it might be good to munch something and you get out some chocolate—the Rapunzel brand—which is really pricey at six bucks for three ounces, but it's soooooo good and you figure you better eat it before it melts. You offer a piece to Peggy and with a grin of total delight, she says, "Ooooo! Thank you!"

You look to Stan and he glances at you two eating, then abruptly looks away like he's gonna barf again.

"I don't think it's seen so much as a problem for people if they are pretty healthy," she says, "it's the older folks, the kids, the seven year olds with boobies—that's the problem—early maturation which was found to be a result of all this chemical stuff in the body."

Yikes, you remember thinking and in your wake/sleep, you realize you really gotta do something about that—

—walking, hiking somewhere in a forest, and around you birds with two heads, frogs with three back feet struggle to get out of your way. A two-headed turtle looks at you warily from beneath a log. What's worse—it's getting near twilight. You don't know where you are, what kind of forest you're in but it's pretty fucking creepy. The trees give way to something strange—like they're trees, but somewhat translucent. You stop and they are made of—*whoa*—you think, *plastic*. You sit on an improbable red bench, the kind you find all over Switzerland but instead of the Swiss Alps around you, it's nature in

Industrial Carpet Drag

chaos, morphing into shapes weird and nightmarish and ghoulish as though evolution is influenced by Mary Shelley of *Frankenstein* fame. You sit and you see someone coming down the trail. You realize it's a seven-year old girl with gigantic boobs and along with her baby—maybe a year old? But with a beard and so well endowed that the diaper barely disguises just how "developed" he is.

Sitting there, you notice the light has become like what you find an hour or so after sunset. The forest has changed now to pines but they are all a cloudy translucent green and it's so eerie.

"Brave new world, eh?"

You turn around. A high-pitched voice with an odd, almost Spanish accent. Then you look down. You freak—almost. Sitting beside you, a spider with—nine legs, one coming out of its back. Ten eyes, all are the color of amber and the color of the spider itself, a shiny blue-green.

"Don't be freaked, my friend. But when you fill the world with chemicals, what do you expect? Evolution goes on and takes what it needs even if—oh well—evolution can't discern if a chemical is OK or if it's a hormone disrupter."

You are still in a state of shock. It has gotten this bad.

The spider scooches about. "Nothing to say?"

You finally say, "I'm totally freaked by what I've seen, and I've not heard a spider talk before."

"Oh, those hormone disrupters," says the spider. "I grew up near a junkyard not far away where computers were being torn apart and scrapped and a lot of the stuff burned to get the precious metals. Lots of plastic stuff in the air. Lots of, I suppose, number 7

123

stuff. Maybe. Maybe other types even worse than 7. Probably more likely."

You ask an improbable question. "Is there something—someone—running this operation?"

"Right the first time," says the spider. "Something more than a someone. Name is Sev N. He—or she—or it—may talk to you maybe about all of this but he—or—it or whatever is pretty entrenched in the way things are. Making money. Doesn't want anything to change. But—if you want to talk to him I warn you—"

You wait.

"Two words you must never, never, never, never say to him because they will come to your mind when you see Sev N."

"What—"

"Don't even THINK of mentioning the name 'Rachel Carson'—or you're an inert additive."

You nod. "OK. So. Where."

The spider motions with the leg on its back. "That way. Up the trail."

You get up, say "Thank you" and continue on. Something large flies by you and you see that it's a dragonfly and it pauses in mid-air to look at you. It's transparent.

"I'm not going to kill you this time," you say. "I felt pretty bad when I did that last time, Mom."

"I don't blame you for being angry," she says. "There's a lot you don't know about our family."

You laugh. "I guess. Tell me?"

"Not now. You are not ready. You'll know when it's time. But not until then. Good try but not now. Sometimes too much knowledge is as incomprehensible as too little. But just pay attention to your memory of Mr. Dinglepood and try some self-

Industrial Carpet Drag

hypnosis. If you are ready, those things will combine and you will get what you are looking for—" a pause and then with real warmth, "seeker. My little seeker. You make me proud, my seeker, my seeker, my brave seeker. We have no guarantees of where our journey takes us. We can only know how proud we are of ourselves for our lives that seek meaning, purpose and love. In the end it's true. The journey is indeed the destination. The journey is guaranteed; the destination—is not. My seeker, my seeker, born of me and like a seed, cast into the world to seek the journey anew. We may talk again and you will be ready to hear what you need to hear to make sense of this all. But for now, Mr. Sev N awaits you."

You are overcome with a sense of something marvelous. That you killed your mother yet she forgives. *Can I*, you wonder, *can I—could I—do that*? Shaking your head, you continue on and in the graying twilight of a world gone wrong, past the forest of plastic, green trees, a structure. You stop. Markings up the side in ounces and the other side, millimeters. A black curved roof and you realize you are looking at a huge plastic replica of your water bottle. You approach, and there is a door with gradations on the side: the top of the door is at the six-ounce mark. As you draw near, it opens and there to greet you is—Mr. Sev N.

☠18.

You are taken aback by the appearance of Mr. Sev N. You've seen many a strange thing and this is just one more of them. He or she or it wears no clothes except for a triangular translucent bikini with a "7" on the front. And given that it leaves little to the imagination you have to wonder why Mr. Sev N wears it at all. You notice that Sev N has breasts and through the translucent plastic, you can see the ovaries as dark shapes. The large penis and the tiny testicles are obvious. "Mr. Sev N," you begin.

"Or Ms. Sev N," Sev N says, "I don't really care. The "Mr." I suppose refers more to the dominant mindset behind industrialization and all the chemicals in the world on behalf of my handiwork, which is extensive."

You take this all in and you are surprised by the gentleness of the voice and the commanding presence of Sev N, tall, muscular yet the features seem also to be a fine blend of male and female. Beneath the transparent skin, you can easily make out all the other organs, which are in different colors of—what appears to be—plastic. You are momentarily mesmerized by the grey-blue of the lungs, just like the carpet in the townhouse, the sage-color of the brains—just like— *hmm*—you ponder—*like the paint*. And the eyes have the same color of—yes, must be coincidental—the pale blue of the AMBLIFOR. And, of course, the ovaries and the testes, yes, the green of your water bottle. The stomach and intestines are the color of lead and the fingernails and the teeth are a curious, mercury-like color while the liver and gall bladder have a really awful, sickly brown-gray color.

"You are impressed," says Mr. Sev N.

"More like distressed," you say. "I never really thought of it before, but just what are all the chemicals doing to us? Are they doing to us what they've done to you?"

But Mr. Sev N laughs. "Oh, no, no, no—" he stops. "What did you ask me?"

"I said," you begin again, "is—"

"Oh, yes, yes, that is correct."

You stop. Something—"—uh—is what correct?"

"What you just said."

"What did I just say?"

"What did I just say. Right?"

"Before that."

"Before what?"

"What I just said."

"Yes."

"Yes—what—?" In all of this, Mr. Sev N looks at you as if totally rational and in control and as if absolutely nothing is out of the ordinary. You've heard a word; it was MaryAnne who told you about when people are hard of hearing or are losing their memories, to look as if they are really OK, they confabulate—come across as if they really understand and there is no problem and the problem, if there is one, must be with you—after all, they're fine. "Of course," you remember MaryAnne saying, "it's fear on their behalf. If they can come across as if having you believe they know what they are talking about, then they are fine and if you have a problem, it has to be you misunderstanding them because, after all, they're fine and there's nothing wrong with *them*."

Ohhhh-kaaaay, you think. *Ohhhh-kay. Here we go again. Mr. Sev N is just another Dr. Morbius—just someone else who not only cannot know what he does not know, but unlike Morbius, where, faced with the inescapable facts facing him, had to finally accept the Monster from the Id was, indeed, his own Id—*

You smile. "Yes," you say.

Ah, you think, *there it is—that flash of fear in the eyes. He thinks he's missed something and is scampering for cues to continue to have you believe he's OK—when, on some level, he knows he's not.*

"Yes," he responds.

"No?" you say. *Oh, boy,* you think, *he's so out of it that he doesn't know how to ask what this is about or what you are doing. He's cueless and clueless—and he knows it and does not want to know it.*

"It's a form of denial," you remember MaryAnne saying, "they are not being consciously manipulative—they know on some level something is not right and it's just too scary to look, to admit there's a problem because of what it means."

And yet, and yet, in their fuck-uppedness—do you excuse them? When people are truly nuts, you do have a loophole: by reason of insanity. That, at times people do wacko things because they are, indeed, nuts, and at that point, by definition, cannot make rational decisions. At those times, they cannot know what they should know. And have no idea of what their impact is on others or maybe even the planet.

You stand there and then you look beyond Mr. Sev N to the crowded room letting in green light, and all around you see plastic furniture and your eyes begin to hurt and—you start sneezing and begin to feel amazingly anxious. You look to your right, a plastic table with an aquarium and in it, you see two headed fish and a crab with one big claw and a small human foot for the other claw.

Mr. Sev N watches you but is not saying anything lest he give himself away that his thought process is— shot. Then you see something really interesting. On the far wall—you kinda have a hunch who that might be. It's a big picture with bullet holes that almost make the image unrecognizable. But you kinda guess it's up there to keep Mr. Sev N upset rather than deal with the reality of what he—and his predecessors— have done and were—and are—willing to do.

But it's just a hunch. A flash of intuition. And you point. "Great poster."

Sev N looks.

"Madam Curie?" you ask. "Ayn Rand?"

Sev N turns back to you. "What?"

You point again. "That picture. The one with the bullet holes."

Mr. Sev N looks again for a long moment. You notice something; his stomach is turning from gray to a gray-red. He turns back to you. Says nothing.

You are now beginning to feel incredibly creepy. *This guy is really good*, you think. *Plays the game better than me.* It also dawns on you that he is really, really out of it; *so* far out of it that there is no possibility of connection which means impossible to know—or care—about—anything or—anyone and certainly not the planet. Maybe so chemicalized that the neural pathways have replaced the organic materials of empathy, compassion, and love and everything else that makes us human. *So, where does that leave me?* You think. *Either leave or—or? Nothing to lose.*

You clear your throat. "Rachel Carson."

Maybe core neural pathways of DDT laid down by the early '60's are so embedded that even they can't be replaced by the chemicals of flame retardants, VOC's, formaldehyde, or everything else in plastics, rugs, and that New Car Smell—but suddenly, all of Mr. Sev N's internal organs go red.

I think he's heard me, you think. What happens next?

It's almost like a PTSD reaction. "COMMIE-FUCKING-BITCH-DDT-IS-FINE-DON'T-KNOW-WHAT-YOU'RE-FUCKING-TALKING-ABOUT—"

It's impressive. You never dreamed words could be put together in such innovative ways.

Flash of movement, the sparkle of light of fast moving plastic and Mr. Sev N leaps to grab a clear plastic AK 47 from right off a black plastic bookshelf crowded with plastic cups, forks, spoons, and plastic bags filled with foam packing peanuts. Grabs the gun and blasts the image of Carson. The bullets, made of plastic hit, shatter and bits of plastic fly, glitter in the light then Mr. Sev N turns toward you—

—you see yourself movin' fast, movin' hard and looking down, your feet are blurred as you sprint and

Industrial Carpet Drag

plastic bullets fly. Up ahead, the trail goes around a bend and in the particular logic of a dream, a phone booth appears. You hop in and close the door while Mr. Sev N streaks on by, AK 47 blazing bullets.

In a minute, heart finally slowing down and you're finally beginning to breathe OK. You look out from the phone booth. He's gone. Then you hear a distant voice from the receiver that has fallen off the cradle: "Deposit fifty cents, please."

☠19.

You exit the phone booth and sit on a plastic red bench. You notice snails, with extra eyestalks and semi-transparent shells, crawling up the legs of the bench, pausing to lick the paint and munch the plastic. And then you notice something else. Your spidey friend is back, crawling up and over the top of the bench. "You said the magic words, didn't you?"

"I did," you say, still feeling mightily shaken and stressed.

"Do any good?"

"Apparently not."

The extra foot on the spider's back bends, flexes. "Hard wired," it says.

"Read something about the controversy," you muse, "back in school. Rachel Carson confronted the pesticide-chemical industrial complex and by extension, manufacturing itself—and boy, the captains of industry didn't want nobody—especially a woman—telling them about what they were doing to the environment."

"Yup," says the spider. "Think it's any different now?"

Industrial Carpet Drag

"Actually," you say, "well—hit and miss I guess—better here—"

The spider looks up at you and you fancy you see imploring in the eyes, a beseeching, but maybe it's your own projection. "Things gotta change fast," says the spider, "things gotta change fast—really fast. Like *now*."

You know. You know. Oh, yeah, you know. And you just don't know how that's gonna happen—yet happen—it must. Now. But—how? You begin to feel like Doc in *Forbidden Planet* after he gets the brain boost from the intelligence enhancer that Krell children used to play with—how Doc's suddenly enhanced intelligence led him to the knowledge of Id—and then he understood what did the Krell in, but Doc didn't live long enough to tell Captain Adams, which led the captain to confront Morbius. Yes. All this evening, all this night, yes, your intelligence has gotten a boost—maybe the dreams that come about at that magic age of 32 plus the VOC's and flame retardants and the booze all combining to amplify a natural process—you don't know, and as you lay there sucking in that multi-flavored townhouse air—

—the scene changes and you suddenly see yourself in what appears to be a hospital and looking down, you are in a white coat—a doctor? You never thought of yourself as bright enough to be a doctor but now somehow, some part of you—does—or at least has that intelligence. *Hm*, you muse, *gotta get one of those brain boosters. I wonder if the Krell survived somewhere and are putting out catalogs*—you look and consider where it is you are now, with patients that line the hallway. You begin walking—an older guy, thin, coughing, in a blue and white striped

133

hospital gown and nasal cannula comes up to you and says, "Please Doc, please, I want another lung transplant. I'll stop smoking this time, I promise—"

You nod, looking at the clipboard on his wheelchair and you see that it would be his fifteenth lung transplant. "We'll see," you say. And you continue on, to the morbidly obese woman, who can't be over nineteen, occupying an extra-wide wheelchair and she says, imploring, begging—"I don't know why those last operations failed—half of my stomach is gone and I've cut way down on my candy bar intake—really I have—now I'm only eating ten a day—"

You nod. "We'll see."

And next is the fellow with uncontrolled diabetes, who is going to undergo an amputation. "Do something," he says, "I don't want to lose my leg! I've done my best, I've gotten my blood sugars down to 600, which for me, is pretty damn good—"

But not good enough, you want to say—but don't. You just nod. You go along, and you just—nod. You nod to the fellow who just can't lose those extra fifty pounds, even though it's probably going to kill him even though he says he walks around the block at least once a week and that should be doing something. On you go, on you go, to the epileptic who won't take medication on religious grounds and who abruptly has a seizure for your entertainment, to the alcoholic who has peripheral neuropathy though, had he stopped drinking six months ago, could have probably escaped it. "Well," he says, desperate, "I was doing fine and I just didn't see a problem—"

And finally you become blind, blasé, indifferent, numb to all you see, for the messages are all the same: *Fix me, make me well but don't expect me to make*

Industrial Carpet Drag

any changes and take responsibility for my own health. Just make we well so I don't have to change, so I can continue smoking and eating and drugging—

You keep walking, you shed your white coat and toss it into a huge and voracious Venus flytrap that closes on it like it's a white moth and you continue on until you come to a hill and looking to the horizon, you also gaze upon the vast sea of humanity, a vast sea of people, of individuals, but collectively, an immense mat covering the Earth, growing, growing, unchecked and you know if you saw such a process in an organism, you would call it a cancer. But each cell, of itself, not having the faintest idea that so many cells kill the host which will eventually kill each cell. *Wow*, you think, *wow*.

You become aware of movement nearby. It's Mr. Dinglepood. He comes up to you and surveys the scene with you. "Quite the something isn't it?"

After a minute you say, "My poor Krell . . . "

Mr. Dinglepood nods. "Freud got the credit for the concept of the Id. My concept of the Monster from the Id as a symbol of the 'Collective Unconscious' was just as valid." Mr. Dinglepood shrugs. "But Freud got the credit. I was seen as too far out there and got ostracized." He takes off his glasses, rubs his eyes. "Hurts."

"Come on," you say, "come on, why won't you say who you really are?"

But Mr. Dinglepood shakes his head. "No," he says softly. "No. I have my reasons. No. Remember, as far as this time, this place, I, Freud, Adler, all the great folks in psychology have been replaced by medication. We are quaint, we were just existential bandages until the Real Truth finally could emerge: we are all electrochemical/magnetic impulses and feeling unhappy or neurotic, or whatever are simply chemical imbalances. It's one of those things that simultaneously has much truth to it—but is also untrue that is *all* we are—and *nothing* more than that. What is missing is the appreciation of the elegance by which the electro/chemical basis of maybe all life forms, including us, becomes aware of itself, its sense of being, of personality and how environment shapes that expression of self." He shakes his head. "Elegant," he whispers, "elegant as it is haunting and ultimately utterly incomprehensible."

Mr. Dinglepood becomes quiet, then just looks out over the vast sea of humanity with you. And then he finally says, "And now, I would guess, it's all a moot point." He waves his hand. "For this desire to reproduce, in part, so that no one will feel like they did not exist, so that they will be remembered, so that generations from now someone will say, 'This was my father, this was my mother, they existed and as long as the line continues, they will continue to exist'—who wants to be forgotten? Who can stand the idea that it will be as if they were never here?"

You suddenly remember an episode from *Star Trek: The Next Generation*, "The Bone Flute"—Captain Jean Luc Picard living out the memories of a vanished people and their message to him, "We were here, don't forget us." You gulp at the memory and how poignant and how beautiful that was.

Then Mr. Dinglepood looks at you directly. "I admire your journey even though you don't understand why it is at this moment, you are experiencing all of this—maybe, dare I say, your unconscious is telling you that you are a whole lot brighter than you think you are."

Industrial Carpet Drag

You suddenly feel so incredibly sad. "Have a hard time believing that—"

"I know," says Mr. Dinglepood softly, and he looks at you with gentle eyes. "I'm going to tell you something that I think you are ready to hear; you may have already heard it. 'Nothing has a stronger influence psychologically on their environment and especially their children than the unlived life of the parent'." He waves his hand again, "So much damage out there and when one is so damaged, one cannot think of the big picture; one is consumed by one's own hurts, rages, the pain, their individual issues—the great collective unconscious, I fear, is too individualized, too fragmented to think in terms of what they and everyone else have in common. Therefore they think in terms of how they are all unique, different, especially in their pain. And given this," he says softly and with the most immense anguish you can imagine, "who among any of these ten billion people would sacrifice their lives so that only one billion lived so that the Earth might heal itself? Who is to decide? Who is to say that right now, nine-tenths of the Earth's population must vanish— so that the Earth, its species and humanity—will survive? That is what must happen. How is that to happen? We have talked of the Krell and just as the story goes, they forgot something—their Id, so we've also forgotten something—the Earth can only sustain so many of us." He laughs, shakes his head. "'My poor Krell . . . they could hardly have understood . . . ' Indeed. Indeed."

You are about to say something but when you turn, Mr. Dinglepood—is gone.

☠20.

You look back to the vast scene before you—people, people, everywhere, all far more similar than different but each one thinking they were far more different—than similar. Ah, yes, advertising: pushing the idea of Individualism to the point of pathology. *Something we all have to learn*, you think, *that we don't want to know: we can't do this anymore. We aren't all that different than those patients I saw, limited in how much insight they had, not to mention taking responsibility. A few not taking responsibility—you can get away with but—but on a global scale—no one wants to change, hence, get rid of global warming so we can keep plundering the planet and grow our numbers unchecked.*

Doesn't work like that. You know it doesn't work like that. But—but—it will change and you know it will change and at horrible cost it will change. Again, again, you feel this immense sadness. You also know you do not know the future and that trends are but trends and in that unknowing, there is consolation. Things can change but—fast enough?

Industrial Carpet Drag

You turn away, and you wonder, wonder about all this and then you find yourself wondering about Mr. Dinglepood's statement. What he said to you about the damage the unlived life of a parent has on their child and abruptly—

—you bolt upright like you've been slugged in the gut—*I was so loyal to my dad and so angry at my mother, yet trying to fix their relationship so they wouldn't split and—failing that—saw myself as a failure—not loveable. And my dad made sure that I knew how important I was to him that no one would come between me and him and mom hurt him and because of my loyalty to him, it meant she also wanted to hurt me.* Oh, my—do you *get* it and that's what you expect of love—to be hurt; love, not to be trusted. And you found ways to prove that to yourself or the perfect people to give you that message.

You get it. Boy, do you *get* it. Trying to fix the family, family came first; fix the family and get their love and you're OK. *Couldn't let love in. Too busy trying to fix the family.* You suddenly don't know who you hate more: your mother or your father or maybe equally, both. You sit there on the couch and it's four a.m. and it might as well be a moment that stretches to infinity and you are reminded of the movie *Like Water for Chocolate*, how Tita got the message she was to serve her mother and that she could not follow her heart. You remember how much you were affected by that movie and now you know why.

You begin crying, crying for what was lost that you can never get back, crying for lost opportunities that loyalty to the family cost you, above all, crying for the lost love of—Michalene, your soul partner who loved you so dearly. And as you sit doubled up on that couch, you say, "Oh, God, Michalene, I didn't know until now. This is what I have had to come to know and I didn't even know I had to come to this place—Michalene, Michalene I am so sorry—" Words fail you. And you cry, you cry and you *cry*.

Finally it is as if the tears have drained whatever part of the ocean of grief that you suspect is still there. And you can't help but think, *Oh, my God, this night. This dreadful, horrendous night.* You flop back on the couch, cover your head with your hands as if trying to hold your head together and you wonder, you wonder, *How can I live in this body over 32 years and only now begin to understand—*

—you feel a presence and it's like MaryAnne, Stan and Peggy are close by, their energy fields soothing you now, as they have guided you, and if their energies could speak, it would be as if they were saying, "Peace, just rest and be at peace. You could not know what you did not know. And now that you know—"

You feel yourself relaxing. *If I had only known, Michalene, if I had just known.* But you, at nineteen, like so many at that age, could *not* know—what you did *not* know.

Slowly you relax even more and you think, *Yeah, for whatever reason I am where I'm at now—it's OK. It's—OK.* How else can you possibly see it? *For if I knew it was to be this way, I would have done everything in my power to change it.*

—you begin to drift again. Warm in the room. You want to open up a window, cool it off but—you start coughing. Then you start sneezing and before you know it—

☠21.

You see yourself lying there on the couch. Your first reaction is that this is an out-of-body experience; it can only mean that you have died. But going up to yourself, you see that you are breathing. *Hoo boy, seeing myself as third-person so what does that make me? A dream? So I am dreaming of myself sleeping but who am I, dreaming this?*

Your head hurts. Too much. You look at the clock on the plasma TV—4:30 a.m. One and a half hours to—well, you usually wake up at six, so one and a half more hours to—dream? To wait until you go back inside yourself? *Will I remember any of this if I am dreaming of myself sleeping? But since I am seeing myself sleeping, I must be dreaming that I am dreaming myself sleeping.* You find yourself pondering. *Going to be boring watching myself sleeping for the next hour and a half.* You watch yourself roll over to turn the TV on then stop—*why not just dream it's on—if this is a dream*—you turn and look outside and the buildings of Seattle are upside down and the moon is a smiley face. No doubt

141

about it. You turn again, seeing yourself on the couch, reaching out and—

—*Bink*—on comes the TV and you think, *since I imagined myself doing that, what is on the TV is all my imagination.* You pull up a chair beside your sleeping self and wonder about the strangeness of this, that, in a dream, you can move physical objects about. You sit. You marvel at how comfortable the chair is. What's this called when all your senses are employed like this, when you are aware of yourself dreaming—*oh, yeah, yeah, lucid dreaming.* You ponder again. Doesn't feel bad, just—strange. *Is this some weird aspect of toxicity or is this just a really lucid dream which is just a dream about sleeping anyway? Or maybe I'm so toxic that this is how it's playing out.* You simply sit for a minute, closing your eyes, then you find you are back in your body on the couch—

—on the TV you see Aasgard Pass, then you are there with Peggy and Stan. Stan has recovered from barfing, you feel better, and Peggy—Peggy in the hiking shorts and those wonderfully tanned legs and that luscious smile—her presence and the presence of Stan—looking around, you see MaryAnne—*what's she doing here?* You didn't know her back when you climbed up Aasgard pass but somehow it's all fine now, it's all fine and now the four of you get your packs on. Time to continue the climb. MaryAnne looks a bit winded but she's still in better shape than you are. You look at her, to those green eyes, that slender body, the shoulder length blond hair and *flash*—it's Michalene. For a second that is eternity, it is Michalene and your heart breaks and then it's MaryAnne again and you suddenly know why you are

Industrial Carpet Drag

with her—somehow, someway, some quality about her is Michalene. Yeah, you got it. *Can't get Michalene but you can sure as hell get someone who in some way is like her*. You smile. Maybe it's OK after all. Couldn't love then, but now—? *Maybe I'm healthier than I thought. Maybe MaryAnne is good for me*. You step through that high plateau of busted gray-white granite, snow fields, high rocky ridges and the endless *gurble, gubble-glurble* of water flowing falling, bubbling, surging, water sparking, frothing, sliding, shimmering, serpentinely flowing over short cliffs, angular flat and ice polished granite, to then gather into slow and quite glacial milk-colored, pale green pools of liquid jade then moving on, on, the sound of water all over again, the cascades of water all around you that gives these mountains the name of water, water water flushing falling flowing in torrents, torment of the guts of life itself and you, walking with MaryAnne and Stan and Peggy and feeling that presence of a connection of soul, of beauty, of being in love with being and being in love with this place here and now and your heart sings with the water, and with the high angelic harmonies of sky and sun and wind and air and there, there, life magnificent and fulfilled.

And you realize in spite of all the pain of that family of the past, in spite of love corrupted, broken and so busted and so twisted and making you do what you had to do to just survive, well survive you did. And maybe in the end, it is the dream, the dream, always the dream that we come to know life's purpose, that of love, beneath this sky and this white sun amongst these stones and little yellow, pink and blue flowers, nodding, bobbing in the breeze beneath the sun, that these moments are that for which we live, that lifts us from the memories of love distorted and corrupted into that which love truly, finally and ultimately is and your heart sings and sings yet sings again.

You come then to a place and you set your backpack down for this is a place to do just that and MaryAnne points to a gently sloping, snow patched ridge and says, "Little Annapurna. Shall we?"

You nod and grin and to yourself you sing, *Little Annapurna yes we shall. Oh, yes, we shall. Under this resolute blue of sky and diamond shining sun, Little Annapurna yes, we shall, oh, yes, oh, yes, yes we shall.*

And the four of you begin that gentle climb up to that ridge, stepping lightly over flat and darkened shards of granite, blasted by winds and baked by sun, yet home to hardy lichens who love it anyway and soon enough, you reach the top and looking out upon the world laid out before you and about you, the vast Enchantment Plateau behind you and 6000 feet down, the gash of Ingalls Creek—

"Wow," says Stan.

"Oh, my," says Peggy.

You just shake your head and MaryAnne just grins, the sunlight makes her teeth as brilliant and white as the snows of Rainier so far south and you all sit, absorbing the beauty of it all, taking it all in, your eyes, your senses, your very skin drinking in this moment and your heart aches to be alive, and aches at this connection, aches at this wonder, aches, aches at the sky and sun and flowing wind as restless as the waters, the sound of which fills the air, the memory of this in your head as if it is now a part of your very being that you will take with you forever.

Industrial Carpet Drag

And soon enough, it's time to go.

"So glad we did this," MaryAnne will say.

And Stan and Peggy just smile and soon you're back to your packs and moving on, down through the grasses, the yet-green larch, to a camp on a small lake and behind a small bluff you will see Annapurna high above and then the tents set up, dinners of Top Ramen stew, the hiss of stove, the water in a roiling boil at this elevation and you sit with coffee, hot chocolate too, and admire the blue of sky slowly fading into moon-filled night and it is a moment that makes your heart break because you realize the beauty of the perfection of this connection, this presence, this sense of love so profound and deep and as quiet as the waters near your place of sleep; a moment to treasure, of serenity, of peace, forever kept so that, in the darkest of times that could come your way, you will say, "I knew of this. I saw and knew of this and knowing this I have all I could ever want. For I have been to heaven and it is indeed here on Earth, on this lovely, lovely Earth."

And dreaming then of your sleeping, within that sleep, a dream, MaryAnne with you, another place and time, on the summit of Del Campo and looking over the icy realm, in the distance you see the smoke of a forest burning, burning and beyond that, the smoke of a planet, burning, burning. And amidst the beautiful icy peaks around you, yet the carnage of the burning in front of you, you understand, as you touch MaryAnne, that love is the answer but with the planet burning, burning, there is not love enough fast enough to stop the Earth from burning, burning—

And in the dreaming of your sleeping, dreaming in that dream of sleep, you imagine yourself with your

dad's father and his brother in the '30's, high on
LaBohn Mountain, looking down on lakes in the
Necklace Valley, "like a baker's dozen" your granddad
always used to say. You, up there with him, with
MaryAnne, your granddad saying they "Felt like kings
looking over our kingdom," the realm and paradise of
the Middle Fork of the Snoqualmie River and in an
aside you say in the dream to MaryAnne, "My love of
nature came from here—here, in this place, my
grandfather knew of life and he wrote, in a haunting
and beautiful narrative of hiking up the Middle Fork
of the Snoqualmie River—writing which I found a few
days ago, as I went through a box of his papers my
fucked-up dad had given me and that I had stashed
in a closet. He wrote, 'There's something that enters
one's blood and makes you say, Boy, it's great!' He
could not know what he did not know, but even so, he
could have those moments, where, with his brother,
coming from such abusive and destructive homes,
they could sill rise above it and looking out over this
Magnificent Wonderscape of rock and snow, of
heather pink and white, and the sound of water,
leaping, flowing, they could still say, "Boy, it's great!"

You want, along with MaryAnne, to say to your
granddad and his brother, "Yes, that's right! Bravo for
you!" and to shake their hands, but as real as they
seem, it is only as ghosts that they exist, though you
are right there with them. You want to say "Thank
you!" to both your grandfather and his brother and
have MaryAnne as your witness and being that of
gratitude, that in spite of the pain you saw your
grandfather endure that was visited upon your dad,
then from him to you (*maybe my dad was the way
he was*, you suddenly realize, *because I bet my dad*

Industrial Carpet Drag

knew I actually liked his dad more than I liked him!)
you nonetheless appreciate knowing that they did
indeed, indeed know of joy and love, as they looked
about, being they as kings, surveying the empire of
rock and ice and azure lakes and the sounds of water,
water, falling, falling, rumbling, crashing, bubbling
burbling all around them, around you in that place,
in that time, looking out over the Middle Fork, then
down to the Necklace Valley over to the Tank Lakes
Plateau—then seeing Stan and Peggy coming up to
also to look upon what your grandfather saw and
feeling the presence, that presence of connection with
life roaring through you like a burning fuse and you
are one with sky and wind and sun, loving the sounds,
the cascading and roaring cacophony of water, water,
flowing wherever possible, that water flowing in this
place, that, on pale gray-granite and busted rock and
you want to introduce Peggy and Stan to your
granddad and his brother at that snapshot in time
but, of course, you can't.

But what you can do is simply point to yourself
and say, "Something worked. It was because they
knew love that they could pass it on in spite of their
pain, they could pass it on, passing on the wonder of
the world, their own sense of being in such majesty
even as they knew little of their own bleak mountains
of pain, they could still come to know and be
transformed by the magic of the natural world and be
alive, be alive, here, this moment, here they knew the
joy of the fullness of being, and being yes, so vibrant
in their youth and oh, so very much alive."

—and in the dream of sleep on the Enchantment
Plateau, you see yourself crying in your sleep, crying,
that in spite of it all, you could indeed come to know

this wonder of this presence of connection of Earth and sky and love and you imagine MaryAnne waking from her sleep and asking you, "Bryce, Bryce, what's wrong?"

And in the darkness you will say, "No, no not what is wrong, it's what's gone *right*. Knowing this sense of gratitude of being here with you and Peggy and Stan, here in this magic and majesty of wild places, having gone through my own torturous terrain, to be here—"

And MaryAnne will whisper to you, "And knowing such a love of life."

"That this," you say, "is as my grandfather said, that it is good. In spite of all his pain, he could say that life was good. What magnificence of spirit, such a spirit my grandfather truly had. Now I can finally see that."

And in the darkness you will feel MaryAnne pull close to you and hold you as you cry from the pain, the beauty that truly living really is. Even as the world is burning, burning—

—you think you come back to the here and now but see yourself sleeping on the couch and you see the tear streaks down your face and you whisper, "—so you are dreaming of this, of what could be and what it is that love can do and where, what directions indeed you can move." You see yourself kneeling beside your sleeping self. "For whatever reason this has come about, be it curse or be it gift, it is up to us to make of it as we will, as we come to know that which we must come to know, however this comes about."

You sit there with your dreaming self. And you whisper, "And now you know what gives you joy and what life could be for you. How fortunate. Will you act on it? If so, how might that come about?"

Industrial Carpet Drag

You then laugh. "You know. That I tell you this—you know. It is but the gift of love and faith. Ah, if only all of us had such power and such vision of the way that things could be. How different might the world become."

You gaze at the plasma screen that you've willed on and you see the world as it is right now: the burning of Australia by wildfires and the smoke billowing and boiling high into the air. You see aircraft twisted, pummeled by unearthly winds that bring them down. You see the polar caps all melting, the sea levels rising and being well into the sixth great mass extinction. You see the world as it is, product of billions of people the world simply cannot hold—

You look back to yourself crying in your sleep. The beauty of the world and being here, the tragedy of a world, burning, burning. And yet you say to the sleeping you, "Remember this. Remember this eloquence of life and love and the poetry of such, for in your heart, you, as we all are, such wondrous poets indeed. We are all such wonderful seers indeed. We are all such Shakespeares and the words of the Koran and the Bible and the Buddha, they are all the language of the heart and soul and mind we speak. If we but spoke! And if we would but hear!"

But you see the tears anew—you see the tear tracks glisten. And you know why; that, in the end, we may be just like the Krell ' . . . who could hardly have understood what power was destroying them.'

☠22.

You awaken with a lurch. *God,* you think, *what the hell—so sad but so—alive—so alive.* You rub your eyes. Wet. Crying? You think, *was I crying in my sleep?* You sit there and try to remember, Aasgard Pass—Peggy, Stan—MaryAnne? *She wasn't there—God how strange, it was like I wish she was, or thought it will be that way—God, I don't know if she even knows what a hiking boot looks like.* You sit there and shake your head. *Wow.* But there was something—you sit there, head in hands. Something so beautiful. *So fucking lovely, like I was taken to—*you just can't put it into words but whatever it was, you know it was lovely and beautiful. Strange how you can have that in spite of stuff like the weather being so scary and horrible—*it's like I'm thinking that we've lost it—is that it? Was I crying from something that I know is beautiful but I know is forever lost? That it?* Then you feel this ache come up, this sadness. *Then there was my grandfather. As screwed-up as granddad was later, he, not my dad, took me out hiking, always was talking about the Middle Fork Country.* You laugh.

Industrial Carpet Drag

Too bad his wife didn't go along. She could have, but didn't want to—wanted to spite him and always just wanted to be away from him. Fine with her if he wandered off into the wilderness and didn't come back for a day or two or three or a week. You feel a chill. *Am I going to end up with someone like that— who really doesn't want to be with me, also just like my mom didn't want to be with my dad—and who's as passive aggressive as my grandmother and my mother were?* You sigh. *Miserable people.* You think, *Just as well Mom and Dad left each other; too bad my grandparents didn't, but boy, how it screwed me up about what I expect of relationships. Wow. No wonder I wouldn't let relationships work. Am I going to wreck it with MaryAnne? Sabotage it like I've sabotaged so many? Is she interested in me so she can play out her crap on me?* You catch yourself. *No, no, don't. Can't go there. That's fear talking—can't—* then you stop. You stop and sit upright. *Wow. Where's this all coming from? I've never had my thinking be so—*you shake your head. *Like I'm seeing connections I've never really been that conscious of before.* In spite of the night and the bad dreams and all else going on, you feel strangely OK. But more, it's felt like no matter what you went through, it was OK, as though there was a sense of love, a presence and you had these dreams. *So weird*, you think, *I cannot figure out a lot of this—maybe it was that last dream—maybe it was the power of love and faith that I'm thinking this way—The Twilight Zone* theme comes into your head—*dee-dee-dee-dee-dee-dee-dum*—and the voice of Rod Serling, "At the signpost up ahead, your next stop, *The Twilight Zone*." *But still*, you think, *that last dream, so powerful,* *haunting and—and so fucking lovely—where the hell did I go? Where did that come from?* You look to the TV. *Don't think I want to turn that on.*

But you do anyway and it's the same old shit about the ongoing weather stuff going on and now New York is being blasted by the same storm that did Chicago in. The picture on the tube is that of a little boy with blond hair and wearing a tee-shirt with Mickey Mouse on the front in his famous cutesy pose of one foot forward, hand behind his back, mouth upon as if saying, "Oh, shucks/golly-gee" and the kid is holding a grapefruit-sized hailstone with both hands and has that look of, "Look what I found and I'm on TV and I'm only five!"

"—and little Andy, what'd you think," says the reporter, leaning near the kid, microphone up close, "when this came through the roof of your house—"

"Whoa," says the kid, "I cou'n b'lieve it. Like, *bam*, and there it was in th' livin' room—"

The reporter looks away from the little boy, leaving him to admire the hailstone or his instant but fleeting celebrity status, hard to say which, but the reporter straightens up, continues, "—report of a tornado touching down in Central Park and some wind gusts with those thunderstorms, hitting 93 mph, hurling baseball-sized hailstones through windows of apartments and skyscrapers. There have been reports of over 2500 lightning strikes just in the last hour. Torrential rains of up to twelve inches an hour completely inundated Washington D.C., stranding cars in lakes in intersections and creating flash flooding which has washed out roads, flooding tunnels— have seen wind gusts up to l2o mph knocking over trees all through the area and even peeling away roofing from the U.S. Capitol building. Power is out for millions and to make it worse—" and the camera focuses in on the fellow, who looks a bit frantic and wild-eyed and he sweeps back hair from his eyes while the scene around him continues to show little Andy staring with fascination at the huge hailstone, "another batch of even worse—" he stops as if saying to himself, "Did I just say that? How much worse can it get?" "—is due to hit Chicago again tomorrow with more tornadoes expected. Seattle has reports of one, maybe two tornadoes touching down unexpectedly while the South swelters under a week long, unrelenting and intensifying heat wave—the temperatures in some places over 110 with 90 percent humidity and the heat related deaths have surpassed 3000—"

You turn the channel. *Something else,* you think, *anything else.*

But you can't concentrate, and everything you see can't hide the fact that—you're scared. You're scared about what you see. You're also stunned and stumped by what to make of this long night and the dreams, the dreams, the dreams. You recall a saying about them—was it Arabic? "To not respond to a dream is like not answering a letter."

I'll talk to MaryAnne, you think, *maybe she might have some ideas* but would you want to talk to her if she was in one of your dreams? You ponder. *Let it rest. Let me just get through the rest this fucking night and get more sleep!* You sit there on the couch, staring at the TV, now on some arts channel. The music is soothing and you see a picture of an orchestra, playing—you think, it's Beethoven. *Pastoral? Eroica?* You decide it's the *Pastoral* and you close your eyes and you find yourself thinking back to the Enchantment Plateau, restful, beautiful. Though you feel yourself relaxing, you still feel strange, light-headed, kinda drugged and you dimly realize that's kinda the way you've been feeling ever since you stepped into this place. Maybe Peggy—maybe MaryAnne is right about carpets and paints—could this stuff really be that harmful? Sick Building Syndrome—you've heard of it but Stan seems—no, he was sneezing too and they haven't been exposed like—you abruptly find yourself so groggy and your head seems to fill with a fog—

—you are on a stage, in a simple garment, fastened by a pin at your shoulders. You are sitting on that stage and your back is to the audience. It's dark, but not like night, more like twilight and somehow, you have this weird sense that you are in a Greek play—and one by one, people, all dressed in the same simple attire, walk on to the stage. Mr. Blaklavach appears and saying nothing, just nods at you and keeps walking to the right of you and stops, looks at you, then folds his hands in front of him. Then Mr. Dinglepood comes on, nods at you and stands next to Mr. Blaklavach. Gazes at you. Then your mother, your father, your grandmother, Doc Adams and Dr. Morbius, from *Forbidden Planet* come on stage as well, some going to the left. Coming up to you and sitting beside you, your grandfather, Peggy and Stan and finally MaryAnne. Then the line of those standing on either side of you begin to rhythmically stomp their feet and clap in time and begin chanting, "The king, the king! Behold! The king approaches." They become silent, step back and all turning their heads to their right, breathe out, "Ahhhhhh—!"

Industrial Carpet Drag

A man comes on the stage, a robust man with a white robe, a deep blue diagonal sash across his chest, held in place near the shoulder by a round gold pin that looks like a sunburst. He comes slowly out to mid-stage, stops, turns his head to look at those behind him, then looks to you and then out to the audience. He takes a deep breath and says, "For I am a just man. And as such, I have witnessed an injustice. As I would wish others to seek justice on my behalf, I, as a just man, must seek justice on the behalf of others. Even if seeking that truth—leads to me."

You sit bolt upright and you know what happens next. "Oh, Geeze," you whisper, "did you have to put your eyes out? You didn't have to do that did you? OK, you killed your dad and married your mom but is that worse than starting war under false pretense? Why didn't Bush put his eyes out? Couldn't you have done community service time or something?" But you know what Sophocles had in mind and for which that was a metaphor: the seeking of absolute justice: as I would seek such justice for others, I must also seek it for myself, even if that means I must—you have this urge to vomit. But you don't; instead you sit and think about this—to be so resolute in seeking the truth and facing it, applying to yourself the punishment. Somehow, you can't see Richard Nixon doing that, nor Hitler, nor Stalin, nor those who manufacture cigarettes or who made the Corvair or sell crack cocaine to kids or who deny that carbon dioxide is fucking up the atmosphere. No accountability. *There's a word for that*, you think, *Sociopathy.*

You listen to the finale of the *Pastoral,* not quite understanding why the music didn't take you to some place other than Oedipus Rex. You glance to the clock on the TV. 5:30 a.m. Outside, sun coming up. Daylight, finally. *Breepbreep*. And the cell phone rattles on the table.

"Yo," the tired voice of Stan. "How goes, dude?"

"Didn't sleep real good," you say. "How you guys?"

"Sleep?" says Stan, "Whuzzat? We got more storms coming today, even worse." Plaintive quality in his voice. "Worse?" he says. "Worse! How the fuck could it possibly be worse? Agh." Then a sigh of immense aggravation mixed with exhaustion. "We gonna be here a few more days, friend," he says. "Peggy is out with her folks trying to get some stuff before the next wave of crap hits. How's it there?"

You glance out the sliders. You laugh. "From where I'm sitting," you say, "you'd never guess anything had happened, anything was wrong. Though you do have a busted window in the upper bathroom from a hailstone."

"Huh—" says Stan. "No shit. Wow. How big a hailstone—?"

"Size of a softball."

Long pause. "You kiddin'?"

"Nope."

"Size of a fucking *softball*?"

"Yeah."

Pause. Then a low whistle. "Well, when you get a chance, can you go out and see what other damage—"

"Yeah," you say, "was just gettin' ready to do that."

"—size of a softball," repeats Stan. "Yikes!" Pause. "Wow! Jee-zus Yikes, yikes, yikes. Well—" obviously not quite knowing where to go next, "—um—well—be in touch here, friend. Otherwise, how you feeling?"

"Weird," you say, "sneezing—had a nosebleed—been having all these weird dreams all night long—"

Industrial Carpet Drag

"Wow," says Stan. "Maybe Peggy is right—I remember sneezing. Well, um—keep the windows open and um—we'll have the place checked out. Maybe we can get some higher class rugs—I think my uncle said that some of the carpeting was ten years old, came out of a warehouse—said he wanted to "Go Green" but apparently that didn't go for the carpeting, but maybe he didn't know—huh—should have—oh, well—go out, look around—see what you find, call back later?"

"OK," you say, "see ya."

Toss phone on the table. *Clatter. Too hard. Don't care*, you think. *Fuck. Maybe I have been poisoned by all this shit.* You sit there, wondering what to do next—sunshine outside, looks nice. Turn on TV—reporter, scene of huge hailstones, downed branches, cars smashed, "—hard to believe that this could be Seattle," reporter says, "never had anything like this before. Geoff Runner has the latest—"

Scene switches to that of the local weather forecaster, Geoff Runner, tanned, boyish and obviously, obviously trying to look OK. "My, wasn't that something last evening?" he shakes his head. "But today should be a lovely day though oddly enough, we may have another intense low pressure area building east of the Cascades—extremely unusual and while we do not—I repeat—do NOT expect a replay of last night's storms over here again—" he shakes his head and laughs, "well we can't rule out the extremely small, I repeat, *extremely* small chance that some areas might see some suspicious clouds and maybe some large hail later today—"

You feel totally paranoid. No matter how Geoff sugar coats it, you are just paranoid. You turn off the

TV, vowing to never, ever turn it on again. Finally you get up, stumble to the kitchen, make coffee and try like hell to act like everything is normal. You still aren't really hungry. At length, you get up, taking your coffee with you, go upstairs and look around again. Yeah, the window in the bathroom off Stan's and Peggy's bedroom is smashed in, all right. The large chunk of ice has melted to an ice-cube size innocent looking rounded lump and you toss it in the sink, then survey the busted glass. *Wow,* you think, *whole bottom panel of the window taken out. Yikes.* You sip the coffee and think you'll come back up later with a box, pick up the glass—gloves, you have to find some gloves. You look around the other rooms. *Ooops. Skylight over hallway cracked. Leaking. Pricey,* you muse. Into the other room, looks OK. But you note, still no way of seeing if shingles are ripped off. Downstairs—you know that's OK. And going to the front door, yeah, tree across the front walk, the hailstones turning into gray white mushy clumps amidst branches in the driveway, and the Subie SVX still looks like a squeezed-from-the-middle car-shaped chunk of soft sausage. Neighbors are coming out to the shared driveway. Out to the street beyond, you can see people looking around, picking up debris, talking to each other. You shake your head. *Yikes. Unbelievable. Yikes.*

You go back upstairs and stand in the living room, holding the warm coffee cup in your hands. You notice you haven't been drinking much from it. It's like you've been holding it more out of security, something warm, safe, sure. You are also aware that you should probably get something to eat.

Well, you think, *might as well get out, get some*

Industrial Carpet Drag

fresh air and see if anything is open and see just how bad things are screwed up. In a few minutes, you are out the door, past your driveway, to the main street and you stop. You stop and you stare: In every direction, trees down, cars smashed by trees and limbs. Big chunks of hail still poke out of slushy melting mounds. Not far away, power lines are draped like long cords of licorice across the road, across cars. *Jee-sus*, you think. You head up Wallingford Avenue, gingerly stepping around trees and limbs and watching out for downed power lines, and in two blocks, you come to the main, east-west thoroughfare, 45th—the few brave souls out by car are stopped by traffic lights out and cars with windshields bashed out from hail and left abandoned, you suspect, as people got out and scrambled for cover under sturdy overhangs of buildings or in doorways. You walk along, hearing the glass from shattered windows *crackle*, *snap* and *pop* beneath your shoes. Finally you come to the new McDonalds which is miraculously open but with a long line forming and you join the line, not knowing where the next place might be that's open and you listen in on the hurried, hushed and haunted conversations around you—"— no one saw it coming how could no one see it coming—?"

"—downstairs when it hit sounded like someone firing cannon balls at the roof and then the porch collapsed. Never seen anything like it, never, never—"

"—the lights went out and the thunder shook the house and then that weird sound—like a train—that tornado—must have been—took the house off the foundations just a few houses over—"

"—lost the windows in the living room. Never seen

hail that big anywhere—I lived for years in Texas and even down there—we didn't see anything like— miGod!"

You look around, not able to attach all the voices to the faces but what you see are men and women looking as if they've been through a war, a mass assault, part of which was the assault itself but also an assault on the denial that anything like that ever, ever happening here, HERE in banana-belt Seattle, HERE with climate so benign, HERE with weather that makes you shake your head at the horrors happening elsewhere except HERE, what the FUCK has happened—oh, those faces, the fear, the anxiety, the incredulity, the pain, the lances of the unpredictability slashing through the safe cocoon of It Couldn't Happen Here and yet—it did. And you consider this as you shuffle forward, and given the situation, as they say, payment for coffee and what food is doled out is by donation only and money seems to be the last thing anyone gives a rat's ass about, including the McDonald's which mercifully has developed a civic soul of "There but by the grace of God go you and I," and you get a coffee and a Breakfast Burger or whatever it was that was not very warm but you take a bite along with a sip of the too-hot coffee and you realize just how hungry you are and you also realize something else: your head is clear. You look around as if you can really see for the first time in a while, with much less of the fuzzy-ness in your brains—you can think. *Clearly*. And you feel this astonishing sense of calmness, of okay-ness. You shake your head in astonishment but then come back to the here and now. You notice there's no place to sit inside. You go outside in the warming sun and you find a low wall to share with others. You sit and drink and eat and wonder, and wonder and think to yourself, *yeah, I have to keep those windows open.* And you realize that in spite of all this crap, you feel pretty good, not only in terms of being fucking lucky, but in spite of all the horrors of this gruesome night, you feel— pretty good—as in well. Healthy. You shake your head. *Has to be the crap in the house.* Yet, as you sip your coffee and take more bites of the Breakfast Burger, you muse, *I learned some things. In spite of it all—don't know why—but I learned some things.* What particularly comes back to you is that memory of being on the Enchantment Plateau with MaryAnne—*OK,* you think, *it's a fantasy of what I hope might happen between myself and MaryAnne.* But also you find yourself really appreciating what your grandfather gave to you which makes you even sadder and more pissed off about your dad. *What the fuck did you give me? Anything I got I got from your dad. God, you fucking jerk—*

"—you OK, young man?"

An older woman and her, you assume, husband, look at you with concern and you say, "Yeah, yeah, wow and yikes and what a night. But I'm OK—" You sip the coffee, "Yeah, yeah, I'm OK." You turn to them. Suddenly you see them as so fragile; not that old, but so vulnerable. She with graying hair and glasses and hazel eyes and he's looking like he just could not believe what he had seen and he's trying to be all strong and look like he can handle any fucking thing except you suspect he suddenly knows he's wrong and he's fucking scared by what that means and he says, "Our dog ran out and got hit by hail and died. Hit by hail right on the head and died. I saw it and I couldn't do a damn thing—" and right then he's the oldest child you've ever seen and it's like you want to go over there and slap your arm around his 60-year-old-but—five-year-old shoulders and say something, "I'm sorry that that happened but we'll go down to the pound tomorrow and you can get another puppy—" but what you say that is actually close enough, since it comes from the heart, all you can say is, "Gee that's too bad. I'm sorry. Looks like a lot of people lost a lot—"

And he nods and in that nod is a "Thank you for hearing me."

"—never been so frightened," his wife continues. She takes slow sips of coffee, holds the white paper cup sans McDonald's logo and simply looks around and finally says, "What a mess."

They sit and sip their coffee, still looking shell-shocked and you drain your cup and stand and say, "You folks be OK? Can I get you more coffee? Something—?" *Something*, you think, *something. Maybe just care and concern and willingness to help,* Guess in the end that's the only something anybody ever wants and really needs.

You see them come back from their PTSD'd dark reverie and say, "Yes, yes, thank you for your concern—we've got family in the area. You?"

You nod. "Be OK. Got friends."

"McCarthers," they say, "Jack and Nancy McCarther. Blue house, corner of Wallingford and 41st. If you need anything, just stop by."

"Thanks, "you say, "Bryce, Bryce Hadfeld. In those new tan townhomes on 42nd and Densmore—the ones with the balconies. Likewise—feel free to come on over. Number C."

You shake hands. *The connection. Someone else*

Industrial Carpet Drag

knows our grief. Someone cares and wants to help. Thank you. Thank you.

Still with coffee you continue on, going East of 45th then dropping down south on Densmore and before long—a crowd of people. A crowd of people looking at the remains of a house—siding wrapped around trees, part of the roof blown across the street, debris hanging from branches and all that remained was the floor and the big brick bulk and vault of the fireplace and everything else, even the chimney—gone, scattered, as they say, to the winds. You gulp. Not that far, not that far at all from where you were—maybe just a block away? And you continue on and stop—another house partially collapsed, much of the roof upside down on the street, cars peeking out from the eaves. Not far at all from where you live. Not far at all. You can see your driveway not too far away, not too far away at all. *Oh, my, God*, you think as you walk by, *oh, my God, that it was that close.* If you weren't shaken before, you sure as hell are now. You dance around the fallen trees, step lightly over a power line, weave around a new, black 2012 BMW, now upside down, and return to the townhouse. You go upstairs and sit down and mechanically take another swallow of the coffee and that it's lukewarm doesn't mean an awful lot. The Breakfast Burger is like a lump of lead in your gut. You glance around to see the sunshine coming through a window. That bright sunshine! Shining through the windows as if it's the most perfect day that ever was and a warm invitation to go out and play. You take another gulp of coffee, put the cup on the table and notice a light blinking on the phone. Picking it up—MaryAnne, and you hit redial—

"Hello," she says, Bryce? Bryce how you doing?"

"Shaken," you say, "got out and walked around to try to see the damage, wanted to give you a call but thought you might be sleeping—"

She laughs. "Didn't sleep very much. Just called a while ago."

"Just got back from McDonalds—they're open, serving free coffee and a gut bomb. God, it's a mess. No one going anywhere,"

"Same here," she says. "Well, anyway, going to get out—see what's going on—were without power but now it's back on. Anyway, maybe I'll get something to eat—then go out—"

"OK," you say, "let's talk later—you'll be all right?"

"Yeah," she says, and there's a long pause and you kinda know what she'd like to say but doesn't, but you kinda know and she says, "Yeah, talk to you later."

"That's good—" you say and you pause and you know what you, too, would like to say but the pause, that momentary silence right now says it best, and you say, "Yeah, that's good. When this mess gets cleared up enough, we can get together?"

"Yeah," she says and you know she knows what you so want to say and she says, "later."

"'Bye."

And you put your hands behind your head, your feet up on a packing box, wondering what to do now—really should open up the doors, the widows, that lightheaded feeling coming back and you sneeze and sneeze and have the sudden sense of being taken down by a grogginess—*the windows*, you think, *the doors—have to open up—what the fuck so groggy—*

—you pick up the phone. "Hi," says MaryAnne, "me again. I just saw the forecast—there's a storm on the east side—they didn't think—" Her voice catches.

Industrial Carpet Drag

You say, "MaryAnne, what? What? I saw something about that but—"

The fear and pain in her voice is startling to hear. "—tornadoes south of The Dalles—Portland suddenly hit by lightning and hurricane-force winds—it's scheduled to—tracked to come up though Puget Sound maybe hit by noon—"

You stand and look out the windows, and notice Seattle is upside-down and a black wall of clouds begin to obscure Mt. Rainier and as you watch, you whimper "Oh, my God—"

—fierce tornadoes rip Mt. Rainier right out of the—

—confusion, images swirl in your head—

—back on that stage again, and Oedipus, with eyes of blood, is led away and slowly the Greek chorus, all those who have appeared in your six hours of dreams produced at age thirty-two by the VOC's and formaldehyde and outgassing of the paint and the Alembifol and stress and nightmare of global warming having turned now fact, no longer fiction, no longer theory, but dropping funnel clouds as you bathe, have coffee with a friend, interrupting *The Daily Show*. No longer just a theory, no, no, now punching holes in your roof or ripping it off, busting out windows—that kind of stress bringing up all the nightmares you thought you never had, maybe thought you lost, had long since gotten rid of, but nope. Just because you've not been aware doesn't mean they're not there—

—all those who have led you to the stage and who have wept for you, loved you, who and have brought you to this place, this time, by whatever means or life events, now depart the stage, leaving you with the presence of those close to you but now, but now, you know, the one last thing remains. For now, your friends must leave as well and as they do, there is from the dark, thunderous applause for a show, allbeit perhaps but a dream, but a show nonetheless, and you think, *this act must end. This is the one thing that remains. How will this act end?*

You now become aware of the night descending, the light dimming until stage and theatre merge into mutual darkness. And then, and then see a light, and moving toward the light you see—

—a child dressed in simple robes. Male or female, it matters not, just a child, hands above a burning candle and above the candle the planet Earth slowly, gently turning, turning, and listening closely you can hear the silent pleas of all life there, knowing if there are other worlds like this one or not, and even if there are, little matter. It is truly all we know. The child sitting there, in a white robe fastened at the shoulder by a simple sun-burst of round pin, hands over that candle, and above the hands, the Earth turning, turning, the flash of seas, the sunlight on the white swirls of clouds, the penumbra and the fading of the day, the coming of the night. The child sitting there, looking at the world, the only world you know and will ever know, the only life you know, and ultimately the only gift you know—the child sitting there, below the outstretched hands, the candle burning, above them, the Earth, turning, turning. The child looks so afraid yet hopeful too; the child looks so long at you and suddenly you know what is so obvious and true—the child you are looking at—is *you.*

☠Acknowledgements

To the early readers of this work, and whose suggestions were so helpful, I thank you: Linda Shepherd, Brian Herbert, Faith Szafranski, Roberta Gregory, and Joel Davis. To Cameron Pearce for his ongoing interest and support of this work. To Vincenzo Bilof for editorial suggestions, Nancy-Lou Polk for computer work and editing this and other books, and Roberta Gregory for final editing. And thanks to Pat Douglas for infinite patience regarding last minute edits of this book which, while delaying publication, nonetheless has made this book far, far better than it would have ever been otherwise. Thank you all!

☠About the Author

Bruce Taylor, aka., "Mr. Magic Realism" writes magic realism (think *Twilight Zone*. His writing has also been described as a cross between Bradbury and Kafka). Recently, he co-edited with Elton Elliott, former editor of *The Science Fiction Review*, the ground breaking anthology, *Like Water for Quarks,* which examines the intersection of the magic realist writing form with science fiction, with such contributors (in the original anthology, Ray Bradbury) as Ursula K. LeGuin, Brian Herbert, Kevin J. Anderson, Connie Willis, Greg Bear, William F. Nolan and many others (now available from baenebooks.com). His book, *Kafka's Uncle and Other Strange Tales,* with introduction by Brian Herbert, was nominated for the &NOW Award for Innovative Writing (SUNY, NY). Another book, *Edward: Dancing On the Edge of Infinity* with introduction by Jay Lake, based on the work by Karl Capek (who gave us the word, "Robot") has received favorable reviews. Bruce is also presently completing the third book of a spiritual trilogy (introduction to be written by Brian Herbert) due out 2014.

All Art is Junk by R. A. Harris

Lana Rivers, a girl with paintbrush hair, is missing and it's up to Lancelot, her cyborg knight, and his bionic conjoined twin, Cilia, to find her before her evil father, a disrespected artist turned mad-scientist, performs a terrible experiment on her.

Cherub by David C. Hayes

Cherub wasn't like the other boys—too slow, too rough—but he didn't deserve what that hospital did to him, and now he will make them pay.

Skinners by Adam Millard

Los Angeles, the City of Angels. At least, that's what the brochure says. What it fails to mention is the earthquakes. Oh, and the flesh-eating creatures lying dormant beneath the concrete, waiting for the chance to surface once again. Their wait is over . . .

The After-Life Story of Pork Knuckles Malone
by MP Johnson

What's a farm boy to do when his pet pig becomes an evil, decaying hunk of ham with slime-spewing psychic powers?

A Lightbulb's Lament by Grant Wamack

A gentleman with a lightbulb for head wakes up in a world full of darkness, hooks up with a beautiful ex-prostitute, and an old man who can heal people; he travels down south to find the mysterious Creator.

The Horror Show by Vincenzo Bilof

A poetry novel—a narcoleptic, amnesiac Nobel Prize-winning poet becomes the subject of an experiment to cure madness.

Gravity Comics Massacre
by Vincenzo Bilof

An absolutely shitty novella involving comic books, aliens, a serial killer, teenagers in an abandoned town, horror-trope dream sequences, and an ending you're going to hate.

Glue by Scott Lange

Sticky bowels and sticky situations.

Ascent by Matthew Bialer

Is the 8 foot tall creature haunting a small town in Iowa in the fall of the year 1903 the product of a hoax and collective imagination or was it one of the first documented paranormal event in America? This epic poem grapples with these questions.

Fecal Terror by David Bernstein

A killer turd is on the loose!

Cucumber Punk by P. A. Douglas

Cucumbers, punks, and lumber. What's not to love?

Terence, Mephisto & Viscera Eyes by Chris Kelso

9 new science fiction stories from Chris Kelso

Bizarro Bizarro: An Anthology

The finest bizarro short stories from 2013.

Captain K and the Bearded Man Boy
by P. A. Douglas

Pat is a super hero and his alcoholic dog can talk. The world must surely be ending.

Day of the Milkman by S. T. Cartledge

In a world dominated by the milk industry, only one milkman survives after a terrible storm sinks all the ships and throws the Great White Sea out of balance.

Moosejaw Frontier by Chris Kelso

An unapologetic disaster of metafiction

Notes from the Guts of a Hippo
by Grant Wamack

A rugged journalist travels to Brazil in search of a missing hippo researcher and the notes left behind lead to something earth shatteringly revelatory.

Industrial Carpet Drag by Bruce Taylor

Chemicals make you do great things!